CODE RED

Dark Tales From Tech

Volume 1

THOMAS MUROSKY

Published by World Where Press
State College, PA
www.owicpub.com

Code Red: Dark Tales in Tech, Vol 1

First Printing 2024
ISBN: 979-8-9914328-0-1 (sc)
ISBN: 979-8-9914328-1-8 (e)

The Internet addresses in this book are accurate at the time of publication. They are provided as a resource, but due to the nature of the Internet, those addresses may change.

Commitment to Open Source: Word Where Press uses FOSS software where available. This book used several FOSS software programs in production including: LibreOffice, GNU Image Manipulator Program, Sigil, Calibre. We used the following open fonts: Charis SIL, Atomic Age, and Hammerhead. Audiobook edition produced with Audacity and Kid3. Images from Pixabay from the following submitters: PIRO4D, geralt, TheDigitalArtist, GDJ

Library of Congress Control Number: 2024946828

Table of Contents

Preamble

Some of my readers might glance through this volume and make a few assumptions about the author. Some would look into the details of many stories and think I am an eternal pessimist. Still others might conclude that I am paranoid. A last group might claim I am a crazy conspiracy theorist as I was recently accused by a company manager who was aghast that I didn't want to receive his store's coupons in the mail!

I promise you that I am neither conspiracy theorist, nor paranoid. Certainly I am also not a pessimist...but I would like to warn my readers and that is the purpose of these stories. While they are fictional (or at least were at the time I wrote them), every story in this book is connected to technology or legal theory *currently in progress* somewhere in our modern world.

Glancing through the titles, our first story relates to artificial intelligence used in ways that are unsettling, but being used consistently with many studies in progress right now. These technologies are not only common in

Asian countries where it originated, but also in the American state of New York where the government is testing this frightening AI application.

Before digging deeper, I wanted to explain the purpose of this book is both to entertain with stories that are close enough to life to be real, but also, as always in my media, I love to learn. I want to teach people to think through the consequences of our technology. It is not that I am a Luddite. I do possess phones and computers...heck, I even use Linux and custom phone ROMs. But often our technology is given to us under marketing fanfare, and not rational thought. We have moved too fast to see *if we can* do something, we never stopped to ask if we *should* do it. Before we know it, a new technology enters our world and the first thought is, "How can this be monetized." Before we know it, stalkers see the cool tracking device designed to silently track your backpack and decide to silently track their victim instead. Henry David Thoreau was correct in saying that our improved technology gives us improved means to reach our deteriorating ends.

I agree with his quote because it aligns with my take on human nature. I realize that my audience may disagree, but I believe that human beings are inherently sinful. Our best attempts at using technology to improve our world (and it can improve many aspects of life), can also be commandeered to increase the evils in this world. To that end, these stories are cautionary tales about how our most praised technologies can be used to cause serious harm.

We need to learn to embrace technology, but we also must safeguard ourselves from its possible harms. Hopefully these tales might impress on my readers more caution about the latest gadget designed to make our lives better. If it gives you enough pause to think through possible consequences, I will have done my job.

To that end, enjoy these stories that hopefully will never come true (though as I write this, an American motor company just patented a technology very similar to what I wrote in Cars Have Eyes).

Digital Madness

I – The Maniac

"Come on son, I won't hurt you," officer Johnson said with de-escalation in his voice.

"NO! I MUST KNOW WHAT'S REAL," countered the strange young man, screaming at the top of his lungs.

The officer lowered his voice, signaling more silence, as the yells echoed to the far corners of the cemetery, being muffled only by the darkness setting in.

"You are not in trouble, but we need to find out who you are. Do you have any ID?"

"I HAVE TO FIND THE TRUTH!" he yelled again.

"What truth?" The officer asked, "We can look for it together if you come with me."

"The truth about everything," the teenager said, finally collapsing in tears.

He lay for a moment sobbing on the ground. Johnson gently grabbed his hand and softly rubbed the top.

"I'll help you find it," he whispered.

He firmed his grip and rose the boy onto his feet. The boy followed along without resistance. Johnson opened the back door of his patrol car and placed the teenager in the rear passenger seat. Once inside his car, Johnson picked up the radio.

"I'm taking this kid to the hospital. He appears to be having a psychotic break. Get CPS there. He is clearly a teen, but I don't know who he is."

The officer placed the car into drive and turned out of the cemetery.

"What's your name, son?" he said in a gentle voice.

"Jeff." he replied.

"Do you have a last name, Jeff?"

"I don't know. I don't know if anything is real anymore."

"Do you know what it might be?"

"No. I don't know what's real anymore."

"Did you try any drugs tonight, Jeff?"

Johnson thought the current string of acid going around town among the teens could cause his outbursts, though Jeff didn't have the dilated eyes, and something seemed amiss about the whole situation.

"Drugs are stupid," he replied, "and these questions will not help us find the truth."

The patrol car stopped in front of a hospital. Johnson picked up the radio to announce the patient's arrival to the hospital staff.

"We don't need to handcuff you, do we?" he finally called out to Jeff.

The officer looked back to see Jeff resting his head on the window with a soft tear gently rolling down his cheek. "Is everything a lie?" he mumbled to the air.

Two large men in white coats approached the car. Johnson got out and met with them outside. Jeff couldn't hear the resulting conversation, but the door opened, and a man named Michael knelt down to be at eye level.

"It's OK son, we will help you find the truth."

He reached out his hand. Jeff looked at the outreached extremity and hesitated for a few seconds, staring at it, as if he wondered what to do. Finally, he reached out his own hand, and they met. The powerful man meekly pulled him from the car, and the four people walked inside.

Johnson poured a cup of coffee and sat at the conference room table with the head nurse and a CPS agent. He shuffled some papers and handed his incident report to the agent and looked between the two people.

"The student ID we found allowed us to get in contact with his mother. She is on the way, and she granted approval for a tox screening. He lives four hours away, if you can believe it."

"What's he doing here?" Johnson asked.

"We have no idea, and the mother doesn't know either. He might be on drugs or something."

The conference room door opened and a man in white hospital scrubs came in and handed a report to the head nurse.

"Thank you," she said, looking down at the paper. Now addressing the room, "there is no evidence of any known drugs. Our initial tests indicate a possible psychotic break. Until the mother arrives, we just need to keep him here and under supervision. We won't have any more ideas without more information. Let's all just get some sleep and handle the rest in the morning.

A frantic woman rushed into the hospital.

"WHERE IS HE?" she yelled.

The security guard threw his paper to the floor and grabbed the frantic woman. Their eyes met, and she gained her composure. She breathed in a few breaths, "I am looking for my son. They said he would be at this hospital."

The guard let go of her hand and said smiled.

"What's his name?"

"Jeff Douglas."

"This way, miss."

The security guard escorted her to the front desk, relaying the information to the clerk stationed in front. She typed in the name and tossed back her hair while the record appeared on the screen. Her eyes gazed at the initial notes and instructions.

"Take the elevator there and head up to the fourth floor. A nursing station is just off the elevator. They will help you up there."

The woman turned quickly and ran to the elevator. Her breath stopped. The elevator directory printed the fourth floor as the psychiatric ward. She stopped to compose her breath before pushing the button for the fourth floor.

The ten-second journey took minutes as random frightening thoughts assaulted her emotions. The elevator door opened, and she rushed to the nursing station.

"I'm Janette. Where's my son!" she yelled before arriving at the station, catching the attendant off guard.

"This way, ma'am."

The nurse led her in the opposite direction from the patient rooms and to the conference center where officer Johnson, Betty, the head nurse, and Rebekah, from child services, prepared for the meeting.

"No, I want to see my son NOW!" Janette screamed upon entering the room and seeing the officials.

"In cases like this," Rebekah started, "We need to have a brief meeting to see what conditions led to this state. You will see him after we go through some preliminaries."

Janette fidgeted under protest and demanded again to see her son until officer Johnson stood up and reached behind his back. Janette analyzed his movements and huffed about it not being fair.

"OK," she said in a huff.

"Does Jeff use drugs?" Rebekah asked.

"How DARE you suggest my boy uses drugs!" the mother yelled back at her.

"It was a question, dear, not an accusation. We need to know what could have resulted in why we're all here."

"No. He would never do that!" she snapped.

"Are there any problems at home?"

"Of course not! Why would you even suggest that?"

Johnson spoke up, fixing a stern look into her eyes, "When we find a frantic kid at night several hundred miles from home, it usually means running away... and that usually means problems at home. So we need a little cooperation here."

"He mentioned something about meeting Grandma. Does she live here?" Betty asked, adjusting her nursing scrubs.

"Why would he want to try seeing Grandma? They talk every Saturday night. I need to get him home so he can get ready to talk to her. Where is he?"

"One more question first. Does Jeff have a history with mental illness?" Betty inquired.

"No. That's crazy!" Janette barked.

The three officials traded glances. They nodded in agreement, as if they telepathically communicated their plans to each other. Betty and Rebekah stood up and motioned for Janette to do the same. The three ladies walked out of the room, leaving Johnson alone with the coffeepot. Betty rattled off status updates and finally informing mom of the condition her son was in when they picked him up.

"Stay here," Betty said, opening the door to room M.

"I have a visitor for you, Jeff." she said.

"Who?"

Janette heard her son from inside the room and burst in.

"LIAR!" Jeff screamed at the top of his lungs. He immediately recoiled.

"NOTHING IS TRUE! ARE YOU REAL?" he continued, yelling.

The screams instantly summoned the orderlies, and they rushed past the three ladies, injecting a needle into Jeff's arm.

"No." he said in fading protest as he nodded off to sleep.

"Come with me," Rebekah said, grabbing Janette's arm.

II – The Mystery

The conference room door burst open, startling Officer Johnson.

"Sit down. We need to be more official now," Rebekah demanded in a tone of dominance.

Johnson, still baffled, traded glances with his colleagues. Betty motioned him outside the room. She quietly explained the scene that transpired when the mother entered the room.

"Clearly, something is wrong," Rebekah started, "Kids rarely burst out like that if everything is going well. If you don't cooperate, we will need to take this case before a judge before you can see your son next. We need some answers."

Janette was silent, then started quiet sobbing, "What did you do to my little boy…"

Her face dropped into her hands as tears seeped through the gaps. Rebekah gently placed a box of tissues on the table. The door opened, and the other two came into the room, taking a seat at the table.

"Grandma appears to be at the center of this. Maybe you should start there," Johnson said. "Is this your mother or his dad's?"

"He doesn't know anyone on his dad's side of the family."

"OK, what's Grandma's name?"

"Grace," she said without emotion, "But I don't see how this relates to anything."

"Tell me about their relationship," Rebekah said, picking up a pen, casually glancing between Janette and the empty paper.

"It's great. They talk online every Saturday," she offered with a smile.

Janette unfolded a perfect relationship fostered over the greatest of technologies. Money being tight and Grandma being a shut in, Janette started doing the calls over Skype before Jeff was born. They shared a perfect digital relationship as Grandma sent cookies, showed her recipes, and watched Jeff grow into a love for games, computers, and other hobbies between his school work. As Janette would put it, the teleconferencing was the best way to build their relationship, show Grandma how Jeff did in school, and stay connected over tight finances and much distance.

Money was always tight, so they could not see Grandma in person, and this always bothered Jeff, but they always had an extended meeting over the holidays. Janette told the authorities that this filled all the need they had to see Grandma, and that Jeff always understood this. He even loved it. He desired their conference calls so much that it drove him into studying computers in his high school courses.

Jeff's eyes slowly opened and focused on Michael sitting in the chair in his room. Jeff connected with Michael over some computer lingo as he measured vital signs and patiently explained to the teenager all the things he was doing in his medical charts.

"What happened?" Jeff said, still waking up from his medicine induced sleep.

"I was hoping we could talk about it, dude. I had to stick you with some sleeping stuff. You went nuts!"

"My mother came in. I remember that."

"Do you remember screaming, 'LIAR' at her? It threw everyone for a loop."

"I don't remember that," he said, embarrassingly throwing his eyes to the floor.

"Can you remember how you got to Ithaca? It would help us find out what you need."

"I took a bus. I needed to get here."

"So you intentionally came to this town specifically?"

"Yes. I was looking for someone. I can't remember who."

Jeff moved glances up at Michael and back down to the floor. He tried to remember what brought him here. Everything he did over the last two days was a blur.

"What's the last thing you remember?"

"I called Grandma. We talked, but something was wrong. Mom was at work, so I thought about the best way to get here. I knew what town she was in, and some of her activities…but I don't know her address."

Jeff paused, looking around the room as if he just saw he was in a hospital room for the first time.

"I don't even know why I'm at the hospital. I feel fine. Can I go home?"

"Afraid not, Jeff. You appear to be having some form of short-term amnesia, and possibly had a psychotic break. We need to figure out what caused that and if you are safe to leave. We have a mandatory seventy-two-hour hold when you're dragged here by the police."

Jeff stared at Michael with odd disbelief. For a moment he was silent, then he finally enunciated each word, "Dragged here by the police?"

"Afraid so, Jeff!" he said with a slight chuckle. The officer's down the hall if you want to talk to him."

"I would, actually."

Michael walked into the room with Johnson and introduced the patient for what seemed to Jeff to be the first time.

"Looks like you are doing better," Johnson said, nodding along with his words.

"Why did you bring me here?"

"You appeared to be having a mental breakdown in a local cemetery. It seemed better to bring you here than to the jail. So we have a mystery on our hands. You don't seem to remember much, and your mom insists everything is perfect at home, but nothing explains why you're going nuts at night in an Ithaca graveyard miles from home. Can you help us figure this out?"

"Yes. I want to go home, but…"

Jeff stopped, not sure what to say or how to say it. The confused words and jumbled emotions blocked his ability to express his thoughts. He paused, looking for the words to say, but couldn't find any.

"Where do we start?" he finally asked.

Johnson recapped the night before and the events that occurred when his mom entered the room.

"There is one person we would like to talk to who seems to be at the center of this," he paused, allowing Jeff to digest the information.

"Who?"

"Tell me about your relationship with your Grandma."

III – The Unraveling

 I love my Grandma," he said, smiling at his words.

"Where does she live?"

"I think she lives here. I think that's why I came to Ithaca." Jeff paused in delight at remembering something. "Her name is Grace. Can you find her? I would like to see her."

Johnson scribbled down some notes on the paper and looked up, nodding in affirmation.

"When was the last time you saw her?"

"We talk every Saturday online!"

"Hmm," Johnson inserted, "When was the last time you saw her in person?"

Jeff thought back for a minute and appeared to be getting more anxious. Michael snapped to attention, ready to grab him if things turned more confrontational. Jeff's eye's caught Michael's, and a slight tear rolled down his cheek.

"I don't remember," he sniffled. "Maybe that's why I came; to see her in real life. I couldn't find her. WHERE IS SHE?" he started getting loud.

Michael inserted himself between Jeff and the officer, grabbing his arm.

"Calm down, Jeff. We'll find her."

Officer Johnson started speaking behind Michael. "If you can tell us some things about her, I'll send someone looking for her. How does that sound?"

Jeff recounted some early memories with Granda. He told the two men that he thinks he last saw her about ten years ago. He remembered taking a bus up to where she lived, a city Jeff believed to be Ithaca. The teenager recounted his earliest memories, the trips to the store, and all the love she showered on him. They were his best remembrances, the ones that filled him with joy during the hard times of adolescence.

"You haven't seen her in person since?" Michael asked.

"No. Think I was five when we last met in person. Then we started talking online."

Jeff recounted the many conversations he had with her over the years. She watched him grow up on the computer screen. She watched his evolution from playing with toys in front of her while mother and daughter talked to an adolescent engaging in actual conversations of his very own with that cherished old lady. They talked about cooking and baking, and then a week later, the cookies they talked about appeared in a box for him on the doorstep.

"Did you ever ask to go visit? Even if you went by yourself on the bus?"

"That was a big fight we had. I must have been about 12."

Jeff recounted the explosive fight. Like most kids, he grew older, and personal relationships flanked toys and trinkets. Jeff wanted to see Grandma in person, becoming less satisfied with their digital meetings. Money was always too tight, mom said. Grandma didn't have the extra money for a trip. She also provided other excuses. Jeff tried to bring up the idea of visiting over holiday breaks, summer vacations, and even over someone's... anyone's birthday. His mom shut down the personal meeting over money, and apparently nothing else. He missed Grandma and vowed to see her as soon as he could earn the money himself.

"That was three years ago?" Johnson asked.

"Yep. Still just Saturday meetings. I like it, but I feel like we need more than relationships through computer screens."

"I agree with that, dude," Michael said. "I'm not sure I would want to only ever see my daughter over a computer screen."

"I slowly gathered information to find her. My mom wouldn't give me the address."

"Couldn't you just ask Grandma?"

Jeff recounted trying to ask her a few times. He sometimes forgot to ask, but when he remembered, she always said to ask his mother. When Jeff said that she wouldn't give it to him, Grandma said that was her decision, and she didn't want to go behind his mom's back. Jeff hatched a plan to learn more about Grandma, so he could investigate where she was himself. He started turning the conversation on her interests and hobbies.

"This is when things started getting…um…weird."

"Weird how, Jeff?" Michael asked.

The more Jeff tried to find out about Grandma, the less she seemed to make sense. Jeff knew she was in the book club at the library and played bingo on Thursday nights, but she would never talk about how she did or any of her friends. Every time Jeff tried to move the conversation toward her hobbies, she would either end the call or change the subject randomly. Jeff learned the titles to some books the club read, but even those titles didn't make sense to him. One book would be a romance, then another about war. None of the books were modern, just historically significant.

"I just started noticing that Grandma appeared to 'glitch out' when I tried to talk to her about her life. She only ever wanted to talk about me."

"What do you mean by 'glitch out'?" Johnson asked.

"Like, when a computer runs out of memory and a program crashes or data in the memory becomes corrupted. We talk about these types of problems in my programming class at school."

Michael was a gamer and understood what he talked about. He clarified what Jeff meant to Johnson, so the officer could better understand the odd phrase.

"Jeff," Michael started, "Do you think Grandma is real?"

The three people stood in silence. Only the equipment in the hospital room made noise while Jeff started looking more and more terrified with each moment.

"She must be. It couldn't be a program. Could it?" Jeff paused. "But I see her every Saturday. We talk! She remembers what I'm doing from week to week!"

"Is this the truth we are looking for?" Johnson said.

Jeff turned his head toward the wall. "I'm done talking now!"

The door closed behind Michael and Officer Johnson.

"Is it possible?" Johnson said, looking at his notebook. "I need to get to the station to look into a few leads. Can you fill in the rest of the staff?"

IV – The Revelation

Johnson opened the door to the local library and headed past the stacks to the librarian's desk.

"You have a book club here, right?"

"Afraid not, officer. Not for a few years now."

"Are there any other book clubs in the area?" Johnson asked.

"None that I know of, and I get asked that question a lot. Is there a book you are looking to understand?"

"No. I'm looking at a mystery. You say there *was* a book club? How many people attended? Do you have records of who showed up?"

The librarian clicked a few keys on the computer and read a date off the screen.

"It looks like the last meeting was two years ago, June 2031. I recall they broke for the summer, but most of the regulars lost interest with other obligations. We have not had a book club since then."

The officer looked over his notes some more. "Can I see a list of attendees?"

"I'm afraid I can't get you that without a court order, officer. You know that!"

Johnson put his notepad away and looked at the librarian. "I don't really need to see the list. I just need to know if one fairly rare first name is on that list. Can you give me a simple yes or no?"

Before she could respond, Johnson started unfolding the unusual case. The librarian listened to the weird idea that the person he searched for may not exist. The librarian stared with unbelief at the story, realizing the officer has already overstepped his bounds in pursuit of the intriguing mystery. She pondered doing the same. Her fingers hovered over the regular attendee chart and fell like a weight rolled over them. She looked at the screen.

"A woman named Grace attended here for years. She died about ten years ago. The only one with that name that ever attended here."

"Ten years, you say?"

"Yes, February 2023 was her last meeting."

"Thank you," Johnson smiled and nodded his head.

Johnson opened the conference room door back at the hospital. Betty and Michael sat next to each other while Rebekah talked to Betty from the left. Janette sat isolated in the far corner, puffy-cheeked casting mistrusting glances around the room. The officer sat at the table and flipped through a stack of papers he carried into the room.

"Ms. Douglas, can you provide an address for your mother?" he started.

"She's in poor health. I don't want you pestering her in her state."

Rebekah caught her eye. "I can go visit her myself. I am on the Adult Protective Services team, too. If she is in failing health, I can certainly look at what help we can provide."

"No. I will NOT allow it!" Janette yelled.

"You will not allow it because she passed away a decade ago," Johnson said softly. "I have the reports here. Maybe you should tell us what happened when she died."

"What do you mean she died!?" Janette said. "I talk to her all the time!"

Johnson flipped through papers.

Here is an affidavit from the librarian that Grace Douglas stopped coming to the book club in February 2023 after she passed away. I also have one from the lady's club at the bingo hall, again confirming that Grace Douglas passed away in February 2023. That is ten years ago. The morgue sent us records of the death, as did the funeral home. We know she died. What we don't know is why didn't you tell us that, and why doesn't Jeff know she passed away? We need some answers here.

"I don't know what you're talking about!" protested Janette. "I talk to her every Saturday!"

"Well, she is from Ithaca, right? You are here? Let's go visit her and settle this," Rebekah said.

Johnson shuffled through more papers. He pulled out one document from the stack and passed it around.

"I heard something about this," Michael said.

He looked at a brochure and a signed consent page from ReBirth, a new project to use data collected by various apps to bring the personality of your loved back in digital form. Michael explained the project to the rest of the people in the room. Microsoft spearheaded it from data collected from their operating system, data collected by using their video conferencing system, and also information gathered from other sources to train an AI model to behave as your relatives. The screen captures from the video conferencing allowed the AI to put an image on the screen.

Michael passed the documents to Betty, who confirmed the signature on the consent form matched the documents Janette signed when she arrived at the hospital.

"Well, Janette?" Johnson said, "Did you sign this form?"

Janette looked at it. The signature matched her own. She nodded.

"I remember," she started sheepishly, "We came up to Ithaca when Jeff was five years old. We stayed with my mom for a week, and it was probably the best week I ever had. Life was perfect, but she also told me that her doctor found a brain tumor. She died within the week, and I was so distraught that I just signed a bunch of papers for the funeral home."

"When did you first use the ReBirth platform?"

"I didn't know anything about it. I just signed the papers, and the company took over her digital accounts. Even before Jeff was born, I talked to my mom every Saturday at 6:00. The Saturday after I arrived home from the funeral, I was in a terrible state. I stared at the computer screen at 5:58 and remembered the times I used to talk to mom. Right at 6:00, a call came into the computer. I answered it, and there she was. She asked how I was, and she asked to see Jeff. I guess I sort of pushed it out of my mind that she actually died, and saw the call come in every Saturday at 6:00 as her. Eventually, I just forgot that she died."

"What about Jeff? Why didn't you tell him she died?"

"I didn't think he needed to know," she said. "He was so young, and the program was so real. By the time he could understand death, I had forgotten all about it."

I Am Watching

I – The Breakup

Jane ducked just as the ashtray brushed past her ear. A soft wind and whiff of ashes tingled her senses right when she heard it smash behind her, scattering itself and the contents to the wall behind her.

"GET OUT!" she yelled at the top of her voice.

"FINE!" Doug yelled back, now screaming in her face. He lunged forward, fixing his foot right before her, causing her to flinch aside.

"Just go," she said again.

Doug turned away and stomped like a toddler up into the bedroom. Jane stood still, breathing rhythmically. She heard rustling around in the room above her head, but she just stood there in total silence. The stomping forced its way down the steps again.

Doug stood at the door and yelled, "If you touch ANYTHING of mine…"

"Just go. Get the rest of your crap later!"

The door slammed shut, and wasting no time, Jane rushed to the door to lock it. It occurred to her later that it didn't matter. He still had a key.

Jane turned her back to the door and slid down to the floor, collapsing into tears. It took ten minutes to collect herself, then she stood up to examine the wall where the ashtray had smashed.

Cindy set her book down and leaned back in the bathtub, soaking her head in the water, when the sound of the phone ringing echoed through the bathroom. She sat up quickly, drying off her hands with the nearby towel before looking down at the phone.

"Hi Jane," she said.

"Cindy, I finally did it. I told that jerk to pack up and get out!"

"Did he hit you again?" her best friend asked.

"No. But I narrowly dodged a flying saucer. He threw his ashtray at me, shattering it against the wall. I'm scrubbing it down now."

"Jane, do not let him back in there, even to get his things. At least not with someone there, like your dad or anyone else you know that can stand up to him."

"I won't. I am sick of being his punching bag," she said.

"What was the fight over this time?" Cindy asked.

"I casually mentioned Jason's name, and he burst out into a jealous rage."

"Jason?" Cindy asked.

"You know, that new guy at work I am training for my old job before the promotion. The promotion and the fact I'm making more than Doug is what caused the last fight...now it's over the guy I'm training. I don't even think he's available!"

"Well, whatever it takes to get that guy out of your life is worth it. You are better than him."

Cindy paused before continuing, "Does he still have the keys?"

"Yes. I am hoping he won't come back."

"You should change your locks. My brother can help you with that. In the meantime, gather up everything of his and get it to him so he doesn't have any reason to come back. If he does, don't listen to any of his false promises of change."

"I won't listen," she said. "I am done with him! But I am going to get off the phone now and pack up everything of his to put in a box near the front door."

"You're off work tomorrow, right? Let's get outta town to do some shopping in Grove City."

"Sounds good. Meet me over here and I'll drive."

Jane hung up the phone and went to the spare bedroom to grab a box. She darted between various rooms looking for anything Doug owned and filled the box with random clothes, a pack of cigarettes he left behind and a few ashtrays. Jane thought about throwing the ashes and all in the box, but had second thoughts, wanting to be the mature one. She meticulously cleaned the ashtray and placed it gently on the top of the box and placed it just inside the front door.

She paused, looking up at the door. Checking the lock, but also realizing that the one person she was afraid of coming in the door had keys. She stood there looking at the door like a puzzle and decided the best option was a barricade. She clumsily pushed the couch back over the old wooden floors until it was flush against the door. After admiring her barricading rearrangement. Satisfied, she went up to sleep off the fight.

Jane didn't have a peaceful sleep. The whole fight and threats of violence kept her up. Each time she dipped into sleep, she saw the face of her tyrant lunging at her. She woke up and rubbed the phantom bruise of last week. It was gone now, but she remembered the pain.

"Don't let him back in," Cindy's voice echoed in her mind.

Jane opened her tired eyes and rehearsed scenarios in her mind. Her daydreams emboldened her beyond what she could ever do in the presence of Doug. If she ever spoke to him in real life as she speaks to him in her fantasies, she might need to visit the doctor. But still she tried thinking of ways to keep him calm but still kick him out. Her restless night slowly dipped into sleep as her exhaustion overtook her racing mind. She dipped off to sleep and finally rested from the fights of the evening.

II – The Road Trip

Jane rubbed the tired out of her eyes and silently looked to the left to see the empty spot where Doug usually slept. Part of her heart missed the companionship. She wondered if she made the best decision in kicking him out. Reality snapped back in when she realized the physical hurts he had caused in her past. She realized she missed someone waking up beside her, not Doug specifically.

"I can go fishing again," she said to herself, confident that she could find a man who treated her better and whom would always be next to her in the morning.

Jane got up and showered away the rest of the tired and placed some music to prepare for the morning. First step was moving the couch back. She huffed in exertion as the couch slid this way, then that. Finally, it rested back where it belonged. Jane next tackled the kitchen duties. She made her usual fruit smoothie for breakfast with coffee as a chaser.

The knock at the door startled her. Jane prepared herself for a visitor, but she wasn't sure who would show up. Jane cautiously looked out the window to know how to prepare herself. She opened the door quickly,

"Nice to see you, Cindy!" She said, stepping out of the way to allow her to enter. Cindy almost tripped over the box while coming in.

"Is this the pile of trash for the garbage man?"

"Yes," Jane snickered, "That's all I found of his."

Jane walked into the kitchen, filling a coffee cup for Cindy.

"I'm still getting ready. Just need to clean up a bit, and then we can head out."

"When is he coming for his crap?" Cindy said to her over the noise of running water.

"Hopefully today. I will be happier when there isn't any reason for him to be here. Speaking of which, did you talk to your brother about changing the locks?" Jane asked.

"He's free tonight after we get back. He will stop by just to look at the door and pick up what he needs before coming over."

The front door opened suddenly.

"Babe, sorry, I can't lose you." Doug realized in a moment that he was talking to Cindy, and not Jane.

"Where is Jane?" He said to her.

Jane heard his voice, and a scowl formed on her face. She stepped out of the kitchen with her hands on her hips.

"I don't want you here anymore. Give me your key and take the box of your things by the door. If anything is missing, send me a text, and I will get it to you somewhere else."

Doug put on a charming, sad smile and slightly tilted his head. "Babe, I'm so sorry. We can work through this."

He put out his hands in a hugging gesture and walked toward Jane. She retaliated with hands out in a stop position. "I just don't trust you," she said. She wondered if she would be so strong in her denial if Cindy were not in the room acting like a fly on the wall darting glances between the two of them.

"Come on," Doug protested.

"GET OUT!" Jane demanded sternly. "Take your box and leave me the key." She reached out her hand for the small object.

"You're making a mistake. You need me, and I might not give you another chance!" He said, elevating his voice while fiddling with his keychain.

"There's your stupid key." He slammed it into her hand, but her resilience didn't let her flinch.

He finally turned his glance toward Cindy, made a frown, and walked out, taking the box. Once the door closed, Jane shook the pain out of her hand.

"Let's get outta here as soon as he leaves," Jane said. "I don't want to be here if he tries to come back."

Cindy peered out the window, watching his truck pull out of the driveway and drive out of view.

"He's gone," she said.

"Great. Let's go."

Doug never let Jane have a whole day with friends, so the women lived up a day shopping at the outlet mall, having lunch in the food court, and visiting every store, a few of them more than once. It was more of a day about therapy rather than a day of shopping. Cindy listened again to a few of the stories of tyranny that Jane had lived under. She heard of the fists and broken furniture, the jealousy, and how he finally exploded over a causal conversation about a new coworker, demonstrating his jealous rage.

Shortly after lunch, they prepared to head back home to be ready for when the new locks to be installed. Jane opened up the door and the two ladies slipped in. Cindy grabbed the phone from the glove box and looked at the screen.

"Do you have an Airtag?" She asked Jane.

"What's that?"

"They are trackers. You can put on your things so you don't lose them."

"No. I didn't know such a thing exists."

"They do, and my phone tells me one is nearby. Maybe someone in the car parked next to us has one on a computer or something," Cindy said. "Let's get going."

She dismissed the notification, and Jane put the car into gear and started driving out of the parking lot.

"That's his truck!" Jane yelled, pointing to a pickup truck, "I'm sure of it!"

There was a figure in the truck, but she couldn't make out who it was from the distance. Her eye trained on the truck as she drove around the parking lot, looping around the whole outlet mall to avoid driving near the jealous ex-boyfriend. Her eyes watched it in the mirror as she drove in the opposite direction. It didn't move.

Jane rounded the mall and headed for the exit, and the truck waited to turn right directly behind her. There was no mistaking the driver for Doug. He watched her as she drove past and kept watching in the mirror as he merged behind her.

"Now what?" Jane said, turning to Cindy for advice.

"Pull into that gas station. See if he follows us."

Jane made the turn. Her eye caught the mostly full gas gauge and pulled right up into a parking spot near the front door. Both women checked the whole surroundings for him. He didn't appear to follow them into the gas station.

"Would he have come here by himself?" Cindy asked.

"Doug? Ha! He's a homeboy. He has a hard enough time going to the grocery store down the street. He is only here because he knew I was here."

"Did he follow us this morning?"

"Possibly. I wouldn't put it past him. But what about that tracking thing you told me about? Can you check for it again?"

Cindy pulled out her phone and navigated to the app to scan for nearby tracking devices. The phone suggested a tracker was still nearby.

"Does he have car keys? Would it be in the car? Maybe in your purse?"

Jane dug around her purse, seeing if anything in there didn't belong to her, but her search came up empty. She started looking around inside the car, but also didn't find the tag. They thought about searching under the car, so they both got out and started looking under the car, feeling around the hard to see corners.

"I found something," Cindy said.

She pulled a magnetic keyholder off a hidden groove under the car and slid open the lid, exposing a little tag.

"Is that it? How can that little thing expose where I am?"

"I don't know how they work, just that iPhone will show me if a tracker I don't own is nearby."

"Great. I don't have an iPhone. How am I supposed to know if I'm being tracked?"

Cindy called her brother to give an update on when they would be home and also to ask for any advice about the tag. Jane used the restroom and bought a pair of coffees for the drive home.

"Sam said to report it to the police, especially since you had a violent outbreak. But he also said to wrap the thing up in aluminum foil until you do."

Her brother explained that the tag uses short wave communication to piggyback location off nearby devices, so foil would stop the device from being able to track anything.

"Sam is heading over there in case Doug shows up," Cindy said.

III – I Am Watching

 Thanks, Sam," Jane said, admiring the new lock, and switching the keys on her ring.

"No problem. Those are good locks. As for the other thing, I would probably report the tracker to the police tonight. No need to wait until the morning."

Jane agreed to do that. She and Cindy both went down to the station and talked to a police officer. Cindy explained the phone alerted her to a tag in multiple locations. They handed the device over to the police and filed the report, suspecting the device of belonging to Doug. She also reported they saw him several miles away from their city, suggesting he was following them. The police filed this all in the report and promised a followup call when they verified the owner of the tag.

Jane still felt uneasy about the situation and even thought she heard the telltale signs of Doug's pickup driving down the road a few times. She wondered if he still checked on the tag and knew it was at the police station. Would that drive him to more extreme tactics? These things spun around in her head until she passed out from exhaustion. The new locks provided little comfort at the moment.

Sunday morning was calm and relaxing at home. Jane tidied up and enjoyed more coffee for breakfast and planned a trip to the grocery store. List in hand, she set out for an afternoon of chores, finally stopping at the grocery store. She hummed a song to herself leaving the store and looked up in disgust to see Doug's truck parked right next to her car. Jane felt a tinge of fear and also an emboldened strength. She decided to not acknowledge him. She kept her eye directly on her car, hitting the key fob and entering the car. Doug opened the door, stepping out, staring at her.

"Jane, we need to talk."

She ignored him, opened the door, and threw the grocery bags into the passenger seat.

"I SAID, WE NEED TO TALK," He yelled, seeing her silent treatment.

She completely ignored him, staring straight ahead, and putting the car in gear. Doug stepped in front of the car, and Jane let loose on the horn and kept slowly creeping ahead. He moved just out of the way, pounding on the car as she passed by, almost running over his feet. He ran a few steps in futility after the car, but turned back dejected toward his truck.

Jane let out the repressed air, and then a small tear rolled down her cheek.

"I can't do this!" she yelled at her empty car. Jane drove and just kept driving. She drove around a few different neighborhoods, taking her time driving down small street after small street. She played the scene at the grocery store over in her mind. Finally, she called Cindy.

"He was at the store when I got out. He was starting his 'I've changed' attitude, but something was different… more violent. I am not sure if he's taking the hint."

"Jane, give him one solid 'You're not welcome here' acknowledgment, and if he doesn't listen, get a restraining order. He is crazy!" Cindy advised.

"That's a good idea. I am NOT letting him back into my life."

Cindy pulled onto her street.

"Looks like I will get to do that now! Doug is waiting at my house!"

"I'll come over if you want, Jane."

"Yes. Please do that. I am going to get off the phone to deal with this. If I don't call back in ten minutes, call the police."

Jane hung up the phone and mustered her courage. She parked on the side of the street in case she needed to make a hasty retreat. Keeping the car running, she opened up her door and stood up, keeping her car between them.

"Jane, I'm sorry. I'm lost without you. Please, let's talk, baby."

"Doug, we are DONE. This is MY house, and you are NOT welcome here. You need to leave right now."

"But, babe, we need to talk this through. We have been through rougher times than this. Our love will bring us together! Can we talk about it over some coffee?"

"No. There is nothing to talk about. We are done. Leave," she yelled back over her engine.

Doug started walking toward her.

"We can't end it without talking. Come on, we need to sit down over some coffee."

As soon as he cleared the back of her car, she got back in and laid on the horn, knowing that neighbors might look outside.

"GO AWAY!" she yelled.

But Doug just kept walking. Before he was close enough to grab the door handle, she threw the car into gear and slammed the gas, kicking up a part of the lawn into his face. She sped off down the road. She reached for her phone and dialed Cindy.

"He's not leaving. I told him to go and he just kept walking closer. I'm going to drive for another few minutes. If he's still there in fifteen, I'm calling the cops!

Jane drove around the block and parked a few streets over to catch her breath. She had just leaned back to close her eyes when the phone rang. She didn't recognize the number and let it go to voicemail. A few minutes later and a voicemail notification beeped. She just stared at the unknown number, pondering the possibility it was her stalker on a new phone. She opted not to check it.

A few more minutes passed and Jane turned on the engine and started back home. The truck was not in the driveway any longer, so she pulled into her spot and collected the groceries. A quick text to Cindy let her know to come over, and she approached the house, seeing a piece of paper wedged in the door. She grabbed the paper and sat down on the couch.

Jane,

I'm sorry. I am a changed man, and I would never hurt you, you know that. We need to make this work. I am owed a conversation before we end it. I will not accept the end of our relationship until we talk. Call me and I will be right over any time. You are forever my babe.

She looked at the note, crumpled it into a ball and tossed it at the wall where the marks from the broken ashtray were still shown. She shook her head and got up to put away the groceries.

Jane met Cindy at the door to go out and look for more trackers attached to the car. Cindy opened up the app and walked around the car. She hit a few buttons and reset the app a few times.

"I'm not seeing any," she said after a minute of walking around the car.

"How did he know I was at the store?" Jane said.

"Might he have guessed you were there?"

"I doubt it. I rarely go to the store on Sundays. And he is not one for shopping. Also, to know exactly where my car is in the store parking lot...it seems more planned than anything else."

Cindy searched her thoughts for more ideas. "Did the police ever call you back?"

"I didn't get a call," but then she remembered the phone call she sent to voice mail. "I got a call that left a message, and I thought it might be him, so I ignored it."

Jane retrieved the phone from her pocket and unlocked the screen. The notification about the voice mail still displayed on the front screen. She clicked the button to play the message and turned on the speaker.

Jane,
This is Officer Murphy, from the Clarion Police Department. I wanted to let you know we retrieved the information about the device you turned in. Can you please call me back or swing by the police department? Thank you.

The women looked at each other. It was the call she waited for, but didn't answer. It had to be the solution, so they opted for a drive to the police station.

"I am looking for Officer Murphy. He left me a voice mail on a device I turned in."

"Right this way, ma'am."

The desk clerk raised the counter gate enough for the two women to follow him back into an office behind the entrance. She knocked on the door that was propped open and walked in without invite.

"Officer Murphy, this is the young lady you were looking for."

The man looked up from his computer, reaching his hand for a coffee cup. He took a sip and set it back down. The stale institutional coffee odor poked at Jane's nose, interrupted by his smile.

"Jane, have a seat. The company that created the tag gave us details about the owner of the tracker you brought it. The stalker purchased it anonymously. We have the attached number, but no one is picking up the phone. We issued an order to find other devices that have been close to the phone number, but don't have that information yet. You think an ex-boyfriend put there it?"

"Yes, sir. Right before we discovered it. Cindy, my friend, discovered it with her iPhone. Once we found it, we saw Doug in Grove City, right where we were shopping. It would be totally out of character for him to be there. I also ran into him at the local grocery store… one he hates going to, parked right next to my car. I told him to leave, but he later showed up at my house."

"I see. We don't have any proof yet that the tracker belongs to him, but we can issue a TPO, Temporary Protection Order, that tells him to stay away from you. There will then be a hearing later to see if the judge extends it. That's what I would do if you think it will be a problem."

"Yes, please, let's do that."

IV – Tools Of The Trade

Jane dabbed her face with just enough makeup to highlight her features. She rustled through her makeup kit for the best cosmetics for a date. Jane hoped Jason was a better man than Doug, and this first date would give her a better impression than she had received working with him at the office. She stood back and took another look at herself in the mirror, fixing a few minor imperfections. She glowed with an excitement she hadn't seen in a long time.

Some last errands in the kitchen distracted her until the doorbell rang.

"Come in Jason. It's nice to see you."

"You, too. I can't believe we're going out. I put together a great evening, so grab what you need. We are heading out to the brewing company for dinner."

"I've never been there, but I heard it is great!"

Jane slung her purse over her shoulder and locked up the house. She smiled at Jason when he walked her to the side of the car and opened up the door for her. She got in, giddy as a schoolgirl on a first date.

"I'm surprised you asked me out," he said while backing out of the driveway. "I thought you had a boyfriend. That's why I didn't ask earlier."

"I had a boyfriend, but he was crazy. I kicked him out and even took out a restraining order because he was so violent. He has not taken a 'No' for an answer and often shows up near the stores I go to."

"Is he really that dangerous?"

"He might be. I have gotten bruises from our fights. The last night he was living with me, he threw his ashtray at me. I dodged it and it shattered against my wall! The next day, we found a tracker attached to my car, and the police linked it to him. He is nuts!"

Jason was quiet, processing the data. In the silence, Jane hoped it was not too much, or that she didn't seem like a crazy person. Jason finally broke the silence.

"How long were you together?"

"About three years," Jane said. "We lived together for about six months. That's when things really got ugly."

Jane paused and reflected on the years with him.

"I guess I should have left earlier, but we always think it will get better. But it doesn't."

"I know that," Jason said. "My sister currently lives with a guy that is a bit crazy. We all see it, and even warn her about the issues, but she always says he promised to change. But he never does."

"That is a lesson I have learned over the last couple of months," Jane said.

The brewery was a pleasant environment for a first date. It was just exotic enough, but also calm enough. They sat a booth against the wall and carried on their conversations, trying to leave the office out of it. Jason scanned the crowd, looking at the bar and noticed a man looking fairly intently at him.

"There is a man over there that appears to be staring at us," he said silently.

"Describe him," Jane said, leaning in.

"He has darker hair, maybe brown. Full a beard, somewhat shaggy, and he is heavyset."

"Oh, God, that might be him."

Jane picked up her phone and turned on the camera in selfie mode, panning the camera to scan the crowd behind her. Nameless faces scanned through her camera until a familiar scowl with angry eyes appeared on the screen. She snapped a picture of him.

"Yep, that is the crazy guy."

"Could he be here on a date?" Jason asked.

"Not a chance! He doesn't go out. Doug's here because I'm here. He is just staring at us."

"Maybe we should pay the bill and leave," Jason suggested.

"No. We need to stand up to him. I have a restraining order, so if he knows it's me and didn't leave, he could be in trouble for being here. I think we should call the police."

"That's not too extreme, is it?" Jason asked.

"What would you do if I were your sister?"

Jason paused, thinking about what Jane said. She was clever, and that increased his attraction to her.

"I have an idea," she said. "I'm going to go talk to that bartender. Watch him to see his reaction. I'll intentionally make eye contact with him, so he knows it's me. If he leaves, fine. But if he keeps watching me or approaches me, we need to call the police to pick him up."

Jason nodded at this plan. Jane stood up, started toward the bar, and looked directly at him, frowning at him. There was no mistaking he knew Jane was there. Finally, Jane reached the bar.

"Excuse me," she said, to get the bartender's attention.

"What can I get you, miss?" he said with a smile.

"Just a little information. That man over there with the beard. Do you know how long he's been here? That guy has been stalking me. I need to know if I need the cops here."

"Oh," he said, "Let me get the manager to look into it for you."

"Jane," a familiar but unwelcome voice called out.

She turned, looking her stalker in the eyes.

"LEAVE ME ALONE" she yelled out.

Her raised voice hushed the restaurant, and she felt the eyes of many patrons resting on them. Jason walked over and stood slightly in front of Jane, hoping an altercation would not happen.

"We need to talk, babe. I'm better than this twerp! You know that!"

"LEAVE ME ALONE" she yelled again.

A couple of burly guys stood up from their drinks and walked over, standing next to Jane.

"I think the lady said to leave, dude," one of them said. His equally large friend cracked some knuckles.

The manager arrived behind the bar just as the scene unfolded.

"Can we all please calm down?" He said, addressing the crowd, "Miss, will you please come with me?"

Jane looked at him and the offer of going behind the counter. She grabbed Jason's shirt and followed. The big friends kept Doug from following them.

"We have alerted the police, and they are just outside. I will ask those gentlemen at the bar to escort him out to them. They are regulars. I am sure they will do it. You can return to your table once he is gone."

"Thank you, and please put their next round on me," she said.

"How did you know she was at the brewery, Doug?"

He looked around in the interrogation room. The white institutional walls did not invite friendly vibes. Nor did the two police officers who were talking to him. He looked down at his cuffed hands.

"I just wanted to talk to her. I know we can work out our problems."

"Do you know the PURPOSE of a restraining order? It is when you can't take no for an answer, and we have to do it for you. There is no talking, so how did you know she was at the brewery?"

"I just guessed she was there."

"How many times have you been there with her?"

"Never."

"Do you see why I don't believe you?"

The officer let the question hang in the air for a while. Another officer came in with a piece of a paper.

"Very good," he said.

Turning to Doug, he held up the paper. "This is a warrant to search your phone. Since you used your phone in the last little stalking attempt, and you don't want to answer my questions, we will just see what the information says."

He let the statement settle into Doug's mind.

"Let's do this. If you tell me now, we can drop a few of the charges. But if we poke around and find the answers ourselves, we will charge you with the maximums! Sound good?"

"OK," Doug said. He sighed in utter defeat. "Get my phone, and I'll unlock it for you and show you."

The officer in the observation room heard the conversation and took the phone, still in the evidence bag, and passed it through the door. The officer set it on the table while the other officer filmed the incident more closely. Doug unlocked the phone and scrolled into the contacts app.

"There is a new setting in the app that if you have their email address and phone number on your phone, you can track the person's movements with the location data on the cell phone. I turned on the sharing feature on Jane's phone when this first rolled out. She is not tech savvy, so she didn't even know this was a feature to turn off. I can now track her through the Google account."

"So she needs to turn off that setting?"

"Yes, and I also would need to delete her contact information from my phone."

"Great," the officer in charge said, looking to his partner, "Now, not only Apple is empowering stalkers, Google is, too."

Central Bank Digital Control

I – The Routine Life

"Good morning, Mr. Schmidt! Will you be enjoying your regular today?"

"Of course, Sally. Some things are better left unchanged!"

"Very good. Just grab a seat and I'll bring it all right over."

William Schmidt took his favorite booth at the diner. The brisk five-minute walk from his apartment refreshed him, and now he prepared for the coffee and donuts he was about to enjoy. A few other familiar strangers filled their orders. He knew many of their names from the eager nature of his gracious host, Sally, the manager of the shop. He was trying to remember if he ever talked to any of them, but a beep from his phone interrupted his thoughts. A notification alerted him to a new article posted to the Daily Digest.

More Conspiracy Theorists Found Bartering Goods, the headline read.

Why won't these people just use the money they give us? He mused to himself.

"Here you go, William," Sally said with a smile. She slide the two donuts on the porcelain plate towards him and gently set the coffee cup down on the table. "You need anything else?"

"No. It all looks perfect as usual, Sally."

William waved his thumb toward her. She smiled and grabbed the fingerprint scanner from her apron. He depressed his print into the device and awaited the friendly beep that the transaction proceeded as usual.

"Sally, do you remember the old days with paper money?"

"Sure I do," she said. "So much fuss over pieces of paper. It's so much easier to process the money now."

"It is. I was just wondering what drives people to want to go back to the old ways. There is another article on the Digest about more nuts trading for services instead of using the money we have to live on. What causes them to keep living like that?"

"I don't know, William. It's so much easier to see our total impact on the environment with our digital dashboard without trying to keep sharing things with each other. I mean, how do they know what their carbon footprint is if it's not recorded in the CBDC dashboard?"

"They're nuts. They just don't care!"

"That's certainly true," she said with a pause, "I need to get that bagel for Mr. Johnson. Let me know if you need anything!"

William scanned the article one more time while sipping his coffee. Another notification overlay the phone screen. He clicked the button to be redirected to his CBDC dashboard. The notification showed the recent transaction and gave options to view balances and deposits. He clicked through and found a notice to redeem his birthday meat credit and another alerting him that The Counsel granted permission to buy a few boards to repair his broken bookshelf. The anticipation of his daily diversion peeked his emotions, and a smile grew across his face as he thought of going to the hardware store to buy his materials.

William clicked the notification for more details. He received some extra money in his account by trading in a few unused carbon credits from the previous year, and still the account projected he would be under his allotment of credits even after purchasing the boards. He finished up his donuts and gulped down the last bit of coffee to prepare for going to the hardware store.

The hardware store was outside his fifteen-minute walk radius, so he opened up the phone app to use a two-way tram credit. He clicked the button and received an immediate approval. He stepped up to the tram station, depressing his fingerprint to use his transport credit. Immediately his phone beeped a carbon credit withdraw from his account. He took a seat, put on his podcast, and watched as the familiar parts of his fifteen minute radius turned into a new block. The new one had all the same shops, just in different locations. It was oddly familiar, yet still unknown. He never walked into that block, for it had nothing his own block didn't have. There was no need to adventure past his fifteen-minute block.

After the unfamiliar block, a large hardware store spanned the entire width of each block. The tram stopped and let off a few people, all going to the hardware store themselves. He noted the return schedule, then he darted into the hardware store like a little kid browsing toys on display. He quickly decided on his purchases and spent the rest of the time walking through the store, looking at all the trinkets available. Of course, he couldn't buy anything other than the approved items, but he could dream about building something with the various forbidden raw materials.

William's phone alerted him that ten minutes remained to catch the return trip, so he checked out and strolled out of the store, drooling over the power tools on display near the exit.

I should have asked for a new drill, he said to himself.

He made it just two minutes before the tram arrived. He smiled with satisfaction at his new boards and passionately sighed as the smell of the hardware store drained from his nostrils.

II – Awakening

He clicked the next episode on the series he had been listening to as the unfamiliar layout of the next fifteen minute block rolled past him through the tram windows. He scrolled through his accounts on the phone while glancing between the phone and the shops. Curious thoughts ran through his mind as part of him yearned to walk this block instead of his own, yet there was barely a need, since they didn't have any unique stores.

The tram ran through the block divider and William stared at the trees going by the windows rapidly. The environmental zone seemed to be about the length of another zone itself. He glanced back down to his phone as his familiar fifteen minute zone entered view. He satisfied himself with his credit budget allotment and slide the phone back into his pocket, preparing to step out into his zone.

He looked down to his boards and breathed delightfully at the different day he had today. He quickened his pace toward his favorite evening dinner place. William stepped through the door into the carry-out line.

"Hi William. Eating on the go today?"

"Oh, hi Julie. I would stay, but I have a few repairs to do." He lifted his bag with the boards in it and smiled delightfully.

She stepped closer and William caught the scent of her perfume.

"You smell nice today," he said. After a brief pause, he continued, "I'll take the v-burger and fries today so I don't make as much of a mess at home."

"Very good. We have some fresh fries coming up right now." She picked up the print payment reader and held it to him. He stared into her eyes as he depressed his print onto the screen. A beep registered the transaction, and he smiled.

"Tomorrow I have a meat credit. I'll be back for a steak. One made from real beef."

"Email us in the morning to make sure we have some beef in. We rarely stock it anymore."

"Will do." He said.

"V-burger and fries to go!" the line expediter called out as the robot slide the pre-packaged meal down the chute.

Julie grabbed the bag and handed it over, slightly brushing her hand across his as she traded off the bag.

"Ketchup?"

"Please."

William sat at his table to eat the dinner. The episode he was listening to finished, and he looked for other to listen to, but a network notification beeped on the phone.

PLANNED TWO HOUR NETWORK OUTAGE COMMENCING AT THIS TIME

William huffed a little, but set the phone down, realizing it was futility to fight against a network outage.

I need to listen to something while I work; he said to himself. An old battery operated radio lay mostly forgotten in a drawer that he kept for emergencies. Most of the stations have long converted to digital network stations, but he thought he might find one or two that still operated.

William opened drawers, rummaging through them, coming up empty-handed and moving onto the next one until finally he found the little radio. He looked at the various ports and power supplies and realized he also still had a pack of AA batteries the radio used. William went back to the previous drawer to extract the batteries and opened the package, inserting the batteries into the device. He turned the knob and raised the volume to a good level. He then adjusted the knob back and forth, looking for a radio station broadcasting.

...meat credits. MEAT CREDITS! Back in my younger days, we could eat meat even if it wasn't our birthday! Our moms gave us treats, not big government!

The announcer paused, allowing dead air to pierce the minds of the listeners at the trailing end of the monologue.

Our next guest used to sit on The Counsel. You know him officially as Silverton, but to us, he is the one with the knowledge of the inner workings of The Counsel.

Thank you, Roger. It's great to be here. As Roger said, I used to sit on The Counsel, and I left because of the corruption, the control, and the hypocrisy. Did you know that The Counsel eats meat nearly every day? They don't want you to eat it, but they do it themselves because they know what you aren't allowed to …that meat is delicious, and even necessary for a healthy body! That is why the scientific journals can't be on the Internet anymore. Sadly, I was the one who pushed that policy. And now they are behind lock-and-key. They know if you read the genuine science, you'll recognize the depth of their lies. But what do I know…I'm just a conspiracy theorist!

William sat listening to the broadcast, intending to work on the shelf, but he instead just held the boards in his hands, captivated. The man on the radio was on the list of banned people. He knew in a moment he must be listening to a pirate station and they must be broadcasting nearby. His first reaction was to turn off the illegal broadcast. Even listening to the broadcast might award him a visit from the peace officers. He reached to turn it off, but he rotated the old knob down to the off position but stopped when it was just barely audible. He heard Mr. Silverton come back on the radio. William laid his head down next to the speaker on very low volume.

Meat is harder to come across, but it is certainly possible to start progressing toward health and personal control over your life with a few steps. If you can find one of the underground markets, we can get you some wheat flour. Such flour is what we used to bake bread with before the ACF became popular. Do you know what ACF is?

That's the key ingredient in the bread we eat every day from the shops. I was even approved to buy a bag recently for a special day of my own.

Thanks, Roger, but I know it's used for bread. I wanted to know if you knew how we named it.

Can't say I know that, Mr. Silverton.

It's short for Arthropod Chitin Flour. Our schools don't teach the genuine science anymore. That's intentional. Arthropod is the group of organisms known better as insects. Chitin is the hard exoskeleton shell. It is not made of starches like wheat flour, what we used to eat. A Glucose Amide is the main composition of ACF. It is not safe for us to eat, but The Counsel has forced it to be the core nutrient in our diet. It's been making us sick and we know that.

That's terrifying, Mr. Silverton.

Indeed, it is Roger. But here we have the steps to help you get healthy. Here in this district, we have an underground store operating only for the next thirty-six hours. It's at the corner of Appleton and Fourth in this fifteen minute block.

The code of operations is 101. Hope to see you there. That ends tonight's broadcast.

William switched the radio off and stared at it for a moment. He thought about the message and asked himself if it could be true. He picked up a sticky note from the table and penned the address.

Appleton and Fourth. And 101.

He wrote them down and stuck the note to the bottom of the radio, hiding it under a few items on the corner of the table. He worked on his shelf in silence, thinking about the illegal broadcast.

III – Second Thoughts

William tossed in bed through the night, thinking about the broadcast and pondering going to the location. He finally nodded off to sleep.

The morning came fast, and he awoke by a few ringing text notifications on his phone. He reached for the phone and clicked through several Happy Birthday notifications. He received another birthday note reminding him of his meat credit, that he had to use in the next three days.

Another message beeped from Julie.

Are you coming in for that meat credit? We have a juicy steak here if you want it.

He hit the reply button.

Sounds amazing. Yes, I plan to come in today about five. See you then.

A thumbs up beeped back almost instantly.

William rolled out of bed and stretched for the ceiling, then bent down and touched his toes, exhaling. His stretching practice kept him healthier than others. At least he thought so. His health could also be attributed to the diet of his former life…a conclusion he came to after thinking about the broadcast.

William got dressed and grabbed his phone. He stepped out of the apartment and walked down the steps toward the cafe.

"Hi William! Happy Birthday!" Sally yelled from behind the corner as he walked in. "The usual?"

William hesitated, then caught himself. "That will be great," he said, feigning a smile.

Sally walked over and looked him in the eye.

"Something wrong?"

"No. I just couldn't sleep last night."

"Old age setting in?" She laughed.

"Nothing like that. I was just thinking, that's all."

"About what?"

"Well, I'm not sure…"

"Come on. Don't you trust me?"

"Of course I do," he said. His mind made up a story. "I was just thinking back to the first time I ever ate a bagel. They tasted different back then. Like they used different ingredients. Do you have the list of your ingredients I can read?"

Sally stood up straight and looked at him with a tilted head.

"As a birthday present?" He said, now smiling for real.

"You know I can't resist you. I'll bring you something to read with your bagels and coffee."

She slid the ingredient list in front of him while he flipped through notifications on his phone.

"Found it. These used to be easier to find. The laws for restaurants used to make these things easy to find and required when someone asked for it, but The Counsel repealed that law."

"Why's that?" He asked.

"Not sure. Maybe they don't want people to question what's in their food."

"Is there a reason to question?" He asked.

"Well, I'm no scientist or dietitian, but the ingredients we use now differ from the old days when I opened this place. The ingredient changes forced us to use extra additives for flavors that used to be natural, and we needed to tweak our recipes to maintain our consistency. I'll leave you to read now."

William reached up his fingerprint to scan the payment device.

"I applied a coupon for your birthday."

William set the phone down and sipped his coffee. He picked up the list and scanned the various ingredients.

There it is. ACF. He said to himself.

He picked up his phone to search out the acronym.

His search query didn't show any results on the first page, but he kept digging deeper. On the fourth page, he found an old text post talking about ACF as a new flour being made from insect exoskeletons. The article date boasted to be twenty years old. He read the research with fascination.

We hope this new flour, made from sustainable cricket farming, might replace the climate devastating effects of growing wheat flour. It's our hope we can replace, or at least supplement, our current flour with this new product for the betterment of mankind.

"It's true," he said out loud.

"What's true?" Sally said from behind him.

"Oh. I was looking up this ingredient online. Do you know what ACF is? It's listed as a key ingredient?"

"Nope. I just use what I have on hand to make it."

"It looks like someone scrubbed the Internet of anything about it. I found an old article from years ago talking about this substance being made of crickets. And they are making us eat this!"

"Yep. Not surprised. But they wouldn't give us ACF if it was bad for us."

"Maybe," he said, taking another bite from his bagel.

William walked down the street, thinking of his breakfast discovery. His mind gravitated himself down

Appleton street, just now passing eighth street. His pulse rate increased with each passing block. He paused his podcast as he approached fourth street. William looked around for any sign of anything out of the ordinary. He looked up and down, even behind him. A small staircase descended beneath the street, and he looked and saw a marking on a door. It looked to be drawn with a silver crayon and simply had two letters: Ag. The marking looked to be styled as the logo of the conspiracy theorists. He knew in an instant that was the location of the shop. His heart rate didn't let him walk down those steps. He quickened his pace, afraid of being seen at this location.

"Julie, do you have that steak ready?"

"I do, William!"

He walked past the people in the takeout line and took his favorite seat overlooking the street so he could watch all the people coming and going about their business. William took in the sights and smells of the restaurant, savoring every moment of his special night out. He glanced around at different tables where people ate their veggie burgers. Most diners focused on their phones as usual, being the only ones in the store. Only one couple was present, a rarity in modern life.

"What sides do you want, birthday boy?"

William looked up and smiled at Julie.

package could make real wheat products for two meals for two weeks for a single person.

He picked up the book again and studied it, finding a meal plan to show him on how to make these ingredients last for two weeks.

Two weeks of meals, for one lunch? He questioned to himself. How could these be so cheap? He momentarily worried that it could be a trick. He now grew paranoid that someone might discover him. Thoughts of flushing the ingredients down the toilet ran through his mind. But he also remembered the bread, the real butter, and he longed deeper for those old times.

William began using the meal kits and reducing his times out at the restaurants. After home cooking for a month, he longed for more home made meals rather than eating out, but his kits only prepared limited meals. He neared the end of his second kit by now, listening regularly to the broadcasts to know where to go for his next kit. Still, he had to preserve his meals, so he rotated through the week skipping random meals.

"Hey stranger," Julie said as he approached the entrance for eating in. "It's been what, three days? Are you cheating on me with Sal's Diner?"

"Not at all. Have not been hungry lately, so I skipped a few dinners."

"Uh, huh? Why the sudden change in your appetite?" She said as he slid into the booth.

"Just that..." He looked around and lowered his voice, "I found an old article on the Internet that talked about the ingredients we have in most of our foods, and how the insects they are using are really not that healthy for us. Kinda kills the mood for the bread and such."

"Careful, William. Don't let what you read on the Internet sway you from the science being taught by The Counsel."

"But what if The Counsel is not basing their recommendations on science?"

"We still have no choice. They are The Counsel."

William fell silent and looked around the room. Returning to his usual voice, he exclaimed, "My usual, please!"

Julie nodded her head, also raising her voice. "Very good, sir."

He scanned through the articles on his phone as he ate his veggie burger, trying not to think about the flour used to make his bun.

"Sir, I have a charge on that account the computer said needed watching. William Schmidt. He is the one in the eighth block with the charge aberrations. It looks like he just returned to his old favorite dining place."

"Thank you, Johnson. Can you pull all his transactions for the last month and get a computer analysis? Meet me at 15:00 to discuss the subject."

"Will do, Mr. Kay"

Johnson clicked on the buttons and the reports for the last month fed into the data analyzer. The computer recommended an extended push to get six months of spending instead, so he clicked the approval button on the screen to allow the computer to access all the data from the artificial intelligence protocol designed for the analysis. He watched as the computer generated a regularity report and then spit out aberrations for the last six weeks.

He collected the data and made his way to the conference room to meet with Mr. Kay.

"Good afternoon, sir. I have the reports here and I have studied the subject."

"What are the results of last month's analysis?"

"I ran them for six months. I first ran the month and gave it to the computer, but the computer suggested a larger report because of a lack of spending consistency. When we did six months, we got some interesting results."

Johnson pulled out the page with the chart showing predictable and consistent spending until six weeks back, when the numbers became erratic. Then he pulled up a graph looking at Internet search results displaying the report on food ingredients just before the erratic spending.

"I already had this website scrubbed from the history and archives. Not sure how it was out there at all. Our intel says that the night before this search, one of the pirate radio stations broadcast. I wonder if he has a radio?"

"Well, it looks like these two restaurants are the regular go to places for him, so we will question them tomorrow. Now we need to find and eliminate the pirate radio stations. Their misinformation *must* stop."

"How can I help with that, sir?" Johnson asked.

"Don't worry about that. Keep an eye on Mr. Schmidt here. We already have a team in place looking at the pirate radio stations."

V – Status Quo

William looked around himself, checking for random viewers, and proceeded down the steps toward the door with the now familiar symbol. The door opened and before seeing anyone, he announced the password of the day.

"Very good. Enter." The voice was not as pleasant as Douglas from his first visit to the shops, but not as bad as the prior host, whose name escaped William.

The room was dark in the front, with only a few candles burning in the room ahead of him. The floor creaked below his feet as he entered the room. William heard the door shut rapidly and several lights turned on. He saw at once several men in suits standing in positions around him. He turned to see one man standing in front of the door.

"We have been waiting for you, Mr. Schmidt," the man opposite the door spoke, forcing William to perform a second about face in as many seconds.

"What do you want from me?" William asked. "I am still offering more carpentry services."

"Oh, we have people for that. What we want from you is to know what you came here for tonight?"

"Who are you?" he asked.

"You know who we are, dear William."

The words rolled silently off his tongue in a mere whisper, *The Counsel*. He stared at the man who was speaking.

"That's right. Don't be afraid, we only want to talk. Please, sit down." The man raised his arm, pointing to a chair awkwardly placed in the center of the room."

"I prefer to stand, sir."

"No. You prefer to sit," the man said in a stern yet calming tone.

His voice compelled William to sit by the words lingering in the air. He fell into the chair and looked around. Another man brought a chair and set it directly in front of William and Mr. Kay sat down, looking William up and down.

"You see, we just want to talk. You are not in any trouble. We are just curious why you came here tonight?"

"I don't know what you're talking about."

"If we nabbed you off the street, you may have business just passing through. But you walked down the stairs. You waited for the door. You said a secret password. And you walked into the door. To what end?"

"I am just looking to buy some food. Is that a crime?"

"It is when the food you buy does not meet our regulatory standards. We just want to keep you safe and healthy. Is that a crime?"

"What if I think the food I would buy here is safer and healthier than what you want me to eat?" William said.

"That's ridiculous. We have done all the scientific studies. We know what's safe and what's not." Mr. Kay said.

"I read the reports about the ACF flour and the problems it caused in all the testing."

Mr. Kay laughed and shook his head. "You mean that discredited report from fifteen years ago? That guy was a kook! Science discredited that report, and the flour we use now is much improved over the arcane recipes we had back then."

Mr. Kay waited for any response, but none came.

"William, we talked to your two friends, Sally and Julie. They both said you have not been in a healthy state of mind for the last month. When we told them we thought your were listening to those misinformation peddlers on the pirate radio station, they both asked what they could do to help you."

"Why did you talk to them? How did you even know they were my friends?" William said, raising his voice.

"My dear Mr. Schmidt, we are The Counsel. We know all. And we work to preserve our world. We could make you disappear, but wouldn't you rather just forget about this misinformation that poisoned your head and go back to the times when we give you all the money you need freely in your account? You have good friends to return to."

He let his words hang in the air more.

"William," he continued, "We want what's best for you. That's why we took your radio."

Mr. Kay reached out his hand, and another man placed a small radio there.

"This is what we found in your apartment. Along with the contraband, which we also confiscated. You see, this little radio was still tuned to last night's broadcast... the one that listed the password. It's not so secret. We let the pirate radio stations run. We record who comes and goes. Some people buy this stuff and it never interferes with their life. But you, William...it has interfered. But we will give you a choice."

William buried his head in his hands before looking up.

"What choices do I have?" he said, dejected.

"Well," started Mr. Kay, "Option one is that we strip your UBI, evict you from your apartment, and drop you off outside the city walls. If you don't want to play by our rules, exile from our glorious society is required. Option two is that this is all a bad dream. You forget about the pirate radio and the unhealthy food, and you go back to life as usual. That is simple. You just take this medicine and you will wake up tomorrow thinking that none of this has ever happened. You will go on living as you did before these misinformation peddlers twisted around your mind. What do you say?"

"Good morning, Sally! I'll take my usual today!"

"Very good, Mr. Schmidt. That's be right out."

William took his seat at his favorite booth and scrolled through the news articles. Sally slid a perfectly toasted bagel and cream cheese onto the table and set a steaming cup of coffee down in front of him.

"Look here, Sally. The news just reported the arrest of more of those pirate radio people. Good riddance to those horrible misinformation peddlers."

"Long live The Counsel," Sally said, holding out the fingerprint scanner to collect her payment.

Gold Finger

I – The Miracle Device

Robert hit the accelerator. His body sank into the seat as his supercharged electric car doubled the speed in seconds, racing through the light just as it turned red. A sly smirk and arrogant chuckle flashed, then vanished. He was running later to the office than he wanted to arrive. Robert lived his life as an overachiever and enjoyed the profits of the game. Acquiring the latest toys, Robert loved showing them off.

His sleek car pulled in his spot and he hopped out, allowing the engine to shut off for itself as he walked away. The doors automatically locked. The car beeped goodbye as Robert approached the office door. He walked up behind Mitchel, fumbling for his keycard with coffee in one hand and breakfast in the other.

"Let me get that for you."

Robert reached his hand out and the green security light triggered on his approach and opened up the lock.

"You should really get your chip before they take away the tax credit, Mitchel."

The colleague nodded his head. "The keycard might be inconvenient, but I like it all the same."

"Suit yourself. It would just make opening the door with full hands that much easier," Robert offered.

"I know, I know," Mitchel said, taking his turn to the right when Robert went left.

Robert continued walking down the hall until he reached the security door leading to his wing. His hand just had to reach for the door, and it swung open.

"Hi Sally," he said, turning into his office.

"Good morning, Mr. Miller," Sally said in a cheerful tone, but keeping her eyes fixed on the computer screen.

Robert sat at his desk and waved his hand near the mouse, and the computer logged in.

"30 emails. Wonderful."

Robert browsed the subject lines, catching his eye on a few microchip automation projects. Since he received his microchip, he had signed up for several product lists of activation options. It seemed he was becoming addicted to finding new things to do with his implant. He felt his whole life becoming easier, and he actively looked for ways to make it easier still.

Robert spent the hour hammering away at emails and revising his upcoming company conference notes. Robert's job as head of security for the office required him to update policies, conforming the company to the recently passed CHIP Act. His presentation was to inform the company about the changes to the security policies to account for the government program rolling out now.

"Mr. Miller, the conference is starting soon," Sally interrupted.

"Thank you. I am just about ready. You can head down if you're ready, and I'll lock up here."

Robert switched off the computer monitor and stretched his hands out before putting his jacket back on. He walked out of the door, closed it and waved his hand by the lock like a Jedi. The light flashed red, and the lock clicked. Robert smiled and turned down the hall.

"Next, we have an update on security protocols. Robert?"

The CEO looked to his left for Robert, who had already started his confident stride to the podium. He pulled a receiver from his pocket and switched it on, setting it on the stand. The presentation already displayed the boring title: CHIP Act and Protocol Updates.

Thank you, Bill. Today we are bringing updated security policies made possible by the CHIP Act. To summarize, the CHIP Act, or Currency Hand Implant Program Act, is not just about money! It allows us to use the implanted chips for any manner of security protocols.

With a smile, he waved his hand over the receiver he previously pulled from his pocket and the slide transitioned. He looked back at the slide and smiled.

See? These microchips are secure and advanced! I can use it in this presentation to advance the slides and move the presentation along. With each wave forward you can see the slide transitions, but moving back, you can roll the slides backwards. This is as revolutionary as Steve Jobs demonstrating the easy scrolling on the first iPhone touch screen.

Robert advanced the slide. It boldly read *About the Act.*

The CHIP Act is a roll-out of a new program to secure banking and currency transactions. People who opt to receive the implants in the first two years before the mandatory period begins will get a tax credit. Employees of this company will also receive a $150 bonus.

Once you have your chip, see the security team to activate your chip with the company servers. Once you do that, you will no longer need to remember your ID badges. Your chip will open all doors and identify you when needed. We will also have information about other things you can do with your chip. You can see me afterwards for some ideas.

Robert concluded his presentation and walked silently off-stage. The meeting ended after a few other company notes and speakers. Employees shuffled back to their duties, with only a few coming to talk to him after the meeting. Sam waited around until he was last.

"Tonight," he said, "Are we still meeting up?"

"Sure, sounds good. Meet me at my place."

"Cool," Sam said. "I have some questions about the chips, but I'll pick your brain tonight."

The day ended as usual and Robert closed up the office after working a little later than anticipated. He walked out and reached his hand for the handle of the car, which popped open and unlocked for him. He slid into the sleek electric car and push the button to power up.

Back at the house, the garage door closed behind him. He approached the door to the house and heard the click of the lock opening. Once he walked in, the lights sensed his hand nearby and turned on. Merely passing by the coffee pot was enough to start a pot of coffee brewing. He glided through the kitchen, loosening his tie as he went. His dress shirt was off before reaching the bedroom, and in a moment he was dressed in casual clothes, waiting for Sam to arrive.

II – Convenience Made Easy

Robert poured a cup of coffee and slouched into his favorite chair. A simple wave of his hand powered up the television. Gestures over the receiver panel on the armrest of the chair flipped through stations as he found something for background noise. Another gesture lowered the volume of the television. He pulled out the smartphone and searched up more ways to automate his life with the chip. After only a few minutes of browsing, the doorbell rang.

Robert slide his phone into the pocket on the chair and extended his hand to the front door. The lock clicked, and he swung the door open.

"Sam, come on in. Can I get you a coffee?"

Sam nodded yes and took a seat on the couch. Robert handed him the cup and sat back down in the chair, waving his hand down to quiet the television even more. Sam looked around at the familiar modern room. Robert had the best of the entertainment systems and sleek furniture to accessorize the digital smart house.

"So, what were the questions about the chip?" Robert asked, breaking the silence.

"I guess, first, does it hurt getting the implant? What does it feel like after you have had it for a while?"

"Well," Robert started, "at first it feels like a shot, and you can feel something under your skin. But after the implant site heals up, you barely notice it. You can feel the implant. It just feels like 'something', but it's not bothersome."

Robert started rubbing his chip, caressing the rice-sized device implanted just under his skin. He could feel it, but he also accepted it as a price for the modern conveniences it gave him.

"So you can feel it now?"

"Yes. It is not irritating…just there. But I think it is a small price to pay for what it gives me."

Robert excitedly bounded out of his chair to give Sam a tour of the powers of the chip.

"Security is easy to handle with the chip. My hand locks and unlocks doors just be being close to them." He walked to the front door and waved his hand back and forth, locking and unlocking the door.

"The best is I never need to remember keys for the house, car, or office. I just walk right up and have access to things I am programmed to access."

Sam nodded. "How is the security, though? If everything is looking for an RFID signal, is not everything also open to more readily hacked?"

"Nah. They encoded these chips with military grade encryption!"

Sam brushed his hand through his hair. "I'm not sure I want to participate in this personally. I think I like the idea of physical keys and such."

"Well, when the act roles fully out, everyone will be required to have a chip…if you want a bank account, anyway." Robert stared him down.

"That might be true, but I still think it is a security risk to do all these optional things. Controlling the TV is one thing, but cars and door locks seem like a security risk to me."

Robert thought for a moment before responding, "Well, the fact this is secure enough for the government to mandate them on bank accounts means they are good enough for everything else, too."

He paused. "Come on, I'll show you a few more things."

Robert walked him into the kitchen, where he showed that a wave of the hand could trigger some settings on the smart coffee pot. Even the refrigerator LCD panel turned on, displaying a camera showing the inside of the fridge to see what's in it without opening the door.

"This entire kitchen is smart and programmed to use the chip. I can turn on the oven, run the microwave, and the chip even controls a few of the smaller appliances."

"What do all these Smart RFID devices cost?"

"They are a pretty penny, if you want them all. But we need to live a little!"

"True, but do you think the average person could afford all this? You're in a high-paying job, but typical people struggle to buy a discount store toaster, let alone some connected smart device."

"That may be true, but I look at what is possible. Besides, if the early adopters like me buy the products, it incentivises the industry to make more and bring down the costs."

Robert smiled, being smug in his position. He also noticed the kitchen blinds were open, so he waved his hand at a little plate on the wall and the blinds slowly crawled shut.

"Let's head over to the bar," Robert finally said.

"Sure thing. Let's drive separate. I'll leave from there."

"Sounds great. I'll see you there."

Robert reached for the door leading to the garage and it unlocked. He opened it up for Sam and stepped out himself. A simple wave of his hand near the wall plate for the garage door started the large door opening. He approached the car, and it opened right up for him.

"So how long before these are mandatory?" Sam asked, now sitting at the bar.

"Stores already need to be compliant," he smiled as he waved his hand over a payment portal on the mahogany. He placed his thumb on the print scanner to verify the drink purchase.

"People don't need them universally for about four more years. But the early adoption phase is always the most fun!"

The man next to Robert perked up. "You have that chip thing?"

"I do," he said excitedly. "It's the best thing I ever did! I didn't need to bring a wallet, ID, money, keys. I only have my phone!"

"How'd you get in here without ID?"

"Public places already have the scanners in place to fully support the chip. I just had to scan that little reader next to the door, and the bouncer gets the OK that I can come in. It saves everyone time."

"You were faster in than I was," Sam chimed in.

"I'm Juan," the man said, reaching out his hand.

"Nice to meet you, Juan. I'm Robert. This is Sam."

"I've been reading up on this law," Juan started. "I'm very curious about how these chips work."

"You're asking the right man," Sam said, taking another sip of beer. "I'm still a skeptic. But what do I know?"

The three men talked for a short period, Juan asking several questions, Sam raising counterpoints, and Robert acting like a chip implant salesman. He talked about the ID verification, payment, and all the little toys he had at home that he controls with a wave of the hand.

"I need to head out, Robert," Sam finally said.

"Sure thing. See you tomorrow."

Robert stood up, shaking his friend's hand. He looked down at Juan, "I'll be right back. Nature is calling me something fierce."

Juan chuckled a little, "Sure thing, man."

He confidently strode into the restroom, fixing his hair in the mirror, and looking to one side then the other. He strode back out like royalty and took his seat back down at the bar. A fresh round of drinks awaited the men as they talked further into the evening about the CHIP Act and all things the chips could do for the users. Juan just kept nodding until Robert neared the end of his second drink.

conversation just as long as he knew it would take for the drugs to take effect.

"Juan is a new kind of criminal. He merges high-end cyber crime with good old fashion burglary. We know from talking to Sam that you like to talk about the chip that you had implanted...God help us all, we all need to get them eventually, thanks to that stupid new law!"

The officer paused, looking down at his hand, dreading the device, and wondering if a lack of his hand might be a better option.

Juan is quite knowledgeable about these chips, and more people are getting them, so he is on the ground floor of his operation. He asked all the questions of you at the bar to get a sense of what you have. He was feeling you out to see if you are a good mark with things to steal. Once he figured out you were the perfect, he spiked your drink and waited for you to leave. He followed you out and caught you as you collapsed.

The officer scrolled through his tablet to a video of the security camera. Robert saw himself collapse into the arms of Juan, who appeared to walk him around the lot, waving his hand near cars. Once a car responded to his chip, it was a simple matter of putting him in the passenger seat of his car.

He might have found Robert's address from the registration, or Juan might have just scanned his hand with the reader device to find out where to go. From there, it was just too easy. He drove to the house, used the garage door opener to open the garage, and walked Robert right into his house. Juan had a team meet him in cover of darkness. Back at the house, they kept Robert unconscious with the drug concoction for as long as they needed to search the place. Once they found a safe, they the just brought the safe to the hand and opened them up. They stole all the valuables and then used the chip and fingerprint to confirm large transactions out of the bank accounts.

"Sorry to tell you, Robert, but that chip you had implanted was used to rob you blind. We will be looking for 'Juan', but he has successfully pulled off this scam in a few states. We checked in on the other cases, and we have yet solved none of them."

The Cars Have Eyes

I – Omniscient Eyes

Boredom overtook the seasoned police officers during the assignment meeting, but to rookie John Davis, the first meeting brought him joy of accomplishment of the goal he set out to achieve: being a police officer. He periodically faded into and out of attention, thinking of the criminals he'd collar and the victims saved by his heroism. His earliest dream to protect and serve had come true. He basked in the accomplishment of his own dream fulfilled. He was about to step out into the world to make it a better place for everyone.

"Davis and Taylor," the chief called out, "Head on down to The Roadmaster to learn of ropes of traffic control."

The two officers stood up and walked out of the room, Taylor giving verbal direction while stepping outside the meeting room. A short walk later and the officers stood before a door reading, TRAFFIC CONTROL CENTER.

"Here it is," smirked Taylor, "The Roadmaster."

The doors opened to more computer monitors than Davis had ever seen. He quickly gazed between monitors displaying detailed maps of San Bernardino county, a screen rolling information too small to see the moving text, and another scrolling through profiles of wanted criminals. The warm institutional room whirred with exhaust noises of a dozen computer cooling fans. Sitting on a rolling chair, darting between several computer monitors, sat a frazzled-looking man with an e-cigarette hanging precariously between his lips.

"What's the news, Masters?"

The e-cigarette straitened to attention while the man shuffled his sneakers, spinning the chair to face the two men entering the room. He gazed through his glasses while puffing the addiction squeezed between his lips. He further loosened his already loose tie and leaned back in his chair.

"That fool Barab is back in our jurisdiction. The Roadmaster is compiling the report on his movements."

"Who is Barab?" Davis chimed in, "and what do you mean by 'compiling a report'?"

Taylor introduced the officers to each other, speeding through the pleasantries. He detailed Joshua Barab's more violent crimes, including the new warrant for armed robbery and assaulting an on-scene officer who had attempted bringing him into custody. As for the report compiling, Taylor left that detail in the capable hands of Ben Masters.

Ben started by walking Davis over to a monitor displaying a map of the county. The roads on the map glowed various colors without apparent rhyme or reason. Ben clarified the color pallet.

"The colors," started Ben, "show the amount of traffic on that road. Light gray roads aren't being used, the red ones have heavy traffic. The ones with the faded borders have police units patrolling on them."

Suddenly, a ping emitted from the speakers near the computer, accompanied by a blip on the main screen. The second monitor focused on the region of the ping and illuminated several dots.

"A police call just came in. That's where the caller is located based on the telemetry data gathered from their phone. The dots are the other vehicles in the area. See how the road border just faded? That's a patrol unit getting close."

A green dot darted into view and slowed to a halt on the map. Ben pushed the dot on the touch screen and a third screen above the second monitor displayed the details of the patrol car.

"Mike is on the scene now."

Suddenly radio static intruded into the conversation, "Masters, do you copy?"

"Masters here. I have one unit on scene."

"It's a burglary. I need a report of any cars that loitered at 352 Maple Street and any that shot away really fast as officers approached."

"Copy that, report commencing… stand by."

Ben unleashed fury on the keyboard and the computer beeped with satisfaction as the report compiled. The details of Mike's patrol car switched instantly to a list of cars, the registered owners, and the proximity to the address.

"Why is that one report red?" Davis inquired.

"The owner of that car is a repeat offender. Like a dog to his vomit, these guys keep going back to a life of crime." Ben said, clicking the report on the screen.

The second monitor formerly displaying the ping location zoomed out slightly and started displaying a single red dot with a caption, **suspect**, posted above it. The computer displayed a counter moving backwards, stopping at thirty-three minutes before the call. It slowed to normal speed, showing exactly when the car arrived, and that it sat across from 352 Maple Street without moving. The computer then rolled ahead quickly to the time of the call, which the computer made a blip as the timer switched from negative to positive numbers. A green dot arrived on the scene about two minutes later, then the suspect's red dot raced out of the view port of the monitor.

"Looks like our guy," said Ben. "The Roadmaster strikes again."

Ben pushed another button and the red dot appeared on the larger county map on the first monitor.

"Dispatch, this is Masters."

"Go ahead"

"Suspect car is a blue dodge hornet, driving west on market street in the 200 block. Likely driver is Lucas Bramble, repeat offender in burglary. Switching to road view now."

Ben clicked on another button and the second monitor now displayed a camera feed from a car. The screen displayed a speedometer indicating 55mph in a

35mph zone just passing the McDonald's on the left. Davis realized in a moment that the car was the suspect's vehicle. The Roadmaster actively displayed the feed from the vehicle's front-facing dash cam. Masters clicked another button and the driver-facing camera engaged, showing a frantic man, sweat dripping from his face, driving erratically while red and blue lights flashed behind him. The photo appeared to match Lucas Bramble.

Several green patrol cars started following from behind, but the detailed information from Ben allowed a few patrol cars to flank the suspect from the oncoming direction. Flashing police lights in the distance forced the suspect to take a hard right turn, causing him to lose control and crash the car into a sign post after an impressive 180-degree turn. Green dots surrounded the now stagnant red dot and Ben saw officers approach the car from the onboard dash cam.

The three officers in the control room traded glances, and the radio chimed in, "Lucas Bramble is in custody."

"And that, Davis, is how we use The Roadmaster."

II – Light Of The World

 Before we hand out assignments," the chief said, starting the daily assignment briefing, "A

dangerous and wanted fugitive has entered our jurisdiction."

The two officers traded glances. They had known whom was to be announced before anyone else; the privileged knowledge of spending the day with the data miner, Ben Masters. Barabs, they both whispered to each other.

The projector screen displayed the same report Davis had seen on the tablet the day before.

"This is Joshua Barab. He's quite dangerous. We know he came into our jurisdiction from vehicle passenger logs, but he appears to have slipped his chip, so we lost him. Barab is wanted for several crimes, including assaulting officers. And those officers can't serve active duty anymore. Apprehend with extreme caution."

"What makes you think he's still here?" an officer asked from the back of the room.

"Connections." The chief answered, "He has friends, family, and associates here. We are monitoring all of them. He's likely planning another robbery, and he doesn't care if people get hurt in the process."

The assignment was patrol duty. Taylor had some ideas to see the further out regions of the county and set up a speed trap so Davis could get some basic traffic stop experience. They stepped out into the bright desert sun and found their patrol car. Taylor took the driver's seat so Davis could get used to the computer without sacrificing driving safety.

"Tomorrow, you drive, but for now, get familiar with the squad car," Taylor said, pulling into traffic.

The patrol navigated roads through the county, leaving the heavier city traffic to find a perch on the back roads, a centurion on the watch. Taylor pointed out different programs on the computer and engaged in small talk about the life of a county patrol officer. A bleep on the monitor interrupted their discussions. Close range communications between cars became required on the heels of the 5G expansion bill, forcing all cars to communicate proximity, speed, and direction to one another. This beep was a special module in the squad car, allowing the early detection of a heavy-footed driver in their immediate proximity.

The computer screen switched to a map view with the patrol car being the center of the map and a red dot approaching their hideaway rapidly. A sidebar on the monitor showed stock footage of a late model Ford, along with a photograph and personal information of the suspected driver.

"Alas…a victim!" Taylor said, hovering his hand over the switch controlling the emergency lights.

The car sped past them without noticing the squad car in the hiding spot behind a large rock. Lights went on, and the patrol car swooped into the road and lit up the speeder. The driver hit the brakes and slowed to a crawl on the shoulder. Both officers opened their doors in unison, approaching the car on different sides. Davis saw the driver matched the photo. They also knew this driver was not a potential threat, allowing them to approach the car with a casual stroll. Taylor engaged with the man from the driver's side while Davis peered in through the windows of the stopped vehicle.

The man was perfectly compliant, but frustrated with himself at the foolishness of speeding down the road. Taylor took the ID back to his patrol car to run it while Davis stayed to talk further to the man.

"Taylor, do you copy?"

Taylor picked up the receiver and radioed back in.

"Taylor here. What's up, Ben?"

"I have a collection of Barab's known associates in your area. Can you check it out?"

"Sure thing. Over and out."

Taylor put the receiver down, and the computer was already displaying a notice about an incoming report. He quickly marked a mere warning to his traffic stop report and pressed the button to load the report. He darted out of the car, running back to the speeder's vehicle.

"You're good to go. Slow it down," he said, almost throwing the ID back at the driver. He then made eye contact with Davis. "We have to go now. We may have just spotted our fugitive."

The officers ran back to the patrol car while the driver counted his fortunes at his warning. The map displayed a red bleeping dot mere miles from the epicenter of their cruiser. Taylor shifted the car into drive and the wheels kicked up dust as he slammed the throttle to the floor. They passed the recent speeder with their lights on and made a quick left-hand turn up ahead.

Davis picked up the radio. "We're approaching the target."

"Careful," Masters reported back, "I'm seeing a few associates of Barab all in a collection. You should wait for backup. We still have the element of surprise."

"Copy that," Davis said.

"We'll make a perimeter here and wait for more troops."

The officers watched the screen as green dots descended on their location from different directions. One car approached right behind them. The car pulled up beside them on the pullout.

"Do you want to take point?" The officer in the other car asked Taylor.

"Sure thing. Let's see what we are looking at before we head in."

He reached for the radio and pressed the button through some static, "Masters, can you see anything on their dash cams?"

"Stand by," Masters repeated.

In The Roadmaster command center, the e-cigarette stood at attention as Ben tickled the keyboards with delight. The screen popped up a view of the house with another car in front of it. The camera in the car showed no useful information. A few keystrokes later and he peered through the second car's dash cam, yielding only a view of the car in front. A third car supplied an equal amount of useless information.

"Taylor, we got nothin'." He continued, "I only see the house and the curtains are closed. Three cars are there, but I don't know how many people are in the house.

Taylor radioed back in, "Alright team, we are not sure what we are looking at other than a collection of Barab's friends. None of them are currently wanted for anything, but last time they all got together like this, a robbery happened shortly after, and Barab injured one of our best officers, reducing him to desk work. We are going to move in carefully."

"Chief here," another voice chimed in, "Taylor, I forwarded you the warrant to print out. All we could get is to search the place for Barab. We have nothing else, so keep your eyes out for anything suspicious in the open. File it in the report."

Davis looked at Taylor. The officers moved in. Starting with Taylor, the solitary house in the desert quickly became a parking lot for police patrol cars. A window blind peaked open, then quickly shut. Silence filled the air until a buzzard called out, echoing the screech in all directions. Taylor and Davis approached the door, hovering their hands over their service pistols.

As they approached, the door opened, causing Davis to draw his gun. A single man stepped out onto the porch with his hands raised. Davis lowered the firearm, keeping it in his hand, but no longer pointing it at the formerly opened door.

"What can I do for you, officers?" the man snarled.

Taylor looked at Davis, who fumbled for the warrant in his other hand.

"I'm looking for a friend of yours. Joshua Barab. Is he here?"

"Nah," the man said, "Not seen him in a while. I think he was in Vegas. Might still be there."

"Who's here with you?"

"Just a few guys drinking some beers and playing cards. We ain't gambling...just some friendly card games."

"We aren't worried about gambling, only about a group of Barab's friends gathered together on a day we hear he's back in town. We have a warrant to search your property to see if he's here. Now is the time to avoid harboring charges if you care to do so."

"You guys are always pesterin' us. What proof do you have?"

"It's all in the warrant. You can read it yourself, but we *are* going in."

Taylor signaled to the other officers. They raised their guns and cautiously stepped in. The officers interrupted a friendly poker game at a musty table, but two empty spots stood smoking cigarettes.

"All you guys need to put you hands on your head and step outside."

The room filled with grunts as the three guys put their cards down. One of them picked up the beer for another swig before belching and walking toward the door. Several officers separated the men and started questioning them on the whereabouts of Joshua Barab. Davis and the other officer stepped into the house to start the search.

A brief commotion echoed further in the bowels of the house, so the two officers darted in that direction. In the back room of the house they spotted their target, Joshua Barab, fighting with a floorboard, but making more noise than he realized he would. They both raised their firearms and barked orders. Their suspect was in custody.

They walked the wanted man outside the house, giving an angry eye to the homeowner, now trying his best not to make eye contact with Taylor. The veteran officer simply grabbed his cuffs.

"You know the drill," he said, arresting the man for lying to the police and harboring a wanted fugitive.

"Yet another dangerous criminal off the streets."

III – The Terror Watches

"Come in Davis," Ben said, still fixing his gaze to the panel of monitors, "I hear you'll be the next nerd."

The department selected Davis for a spot in the rotation for The Roadmaster to relieve Ben when he needed days off. He eagerly wanted to learn the system that sent leads to patrol units. His fantasies imagining him being the ones making calls to officers in the field, taking point in the capture of fugitives. He knew in his heart it was arrogance, but he really didn't care.

Ben motioned to the corner where two more chairs sat clustered together to escape the fury of the computer master rolling from station to station. The way Ben pushed himself from one spot to another was as impressive as an Olympic sport.

"First, over here," he beckoned to the computer rookie to the present station, "This one is our wanted database. It shows the people with active warrants, but also gives us their known associates, and any cars attached to their name. The new laws allow us to click the button to see if there is a vehicle belonging to them in our county. As long as it is within our geofence, we got 'em."

Ben pulled up the first warrant name on the screen. Timothy Rochester was wanted for unpaid speeding tickets. He clicked the button to see the details of his car. The computer on the next station over displayed a blip on the map displaying the current location of the car in the county geofence.

"See, if an officer is looking for something to do, I could ping this, show the location, and send a patrol officer over to check it out. He might collar a warrant!"

"That seems invasive, doesn't it?" Davis sheepishly asked.

"Well, if they're in the system, it is a matter of time until we get to 'em. Might as well be sooner than later. We can sort by major warrants, and the computer will blip if a new warrantee enters our geofence."

Davis scrolled through the list of names with active warrants, clicking on a few to see if they were on the map. A few of the names pinged a dot, others didn't. He kept scrolling through, poking as he went.

"You've already seen this one," Ben waving at the primary computer with the central maps. He continued, "So over here is the records database."

Davis rolled his chair over more to the right to the last computer in the room. A computer interface displayed a form field with a readout overhead, INPUT NAME.

"This one takes the most trust of all. It lists the DMV records with all the other pertinent information about the subject being searched. It shows warrant status, address, and any other records we might know."

"What do you mean, 'we might know'?" Davis asked, on the edge of curiosity.

"Ever hear of Palantir?"

"No. What is it?"

"That tech investor guy found it as an aid to police departments and other government contracts. It's a specialized web scrapper that goes through the Internet, social media posts, and other public records looking for information on anyone we input into the computer. It gives us a better picture of who someone is."

A tinge of disgust shivered up Davis's spine. He had nightmares of such things since the Snowden revelations, but didn't realize something like this happened in the civilian world.

"How is that legal?"

"Because the government doesn't do any of the searches or store the information, it satisfies the fourth the amendment. We don't own that database, we just pay for access to it. A bill floated through Congress a few years ago to end such partnerships, but the opponents defeated it, so we can use all the data from this system we want. Just don't look up any ex-girlfriends," Masters concluded with a smirk.

Davis hated the violation before his eyes, yet he stood tempted all the same. He so longed to grab the keyboard and cram in a few names. What would be the result if he knew where the beauties and the beasts of his past life had gone to? Davis stared into the field, mesmerized by the blinking cursor, but paralyzed by the fear of being found out.

"Have any questions?" Masters broke the spell and redirected Davis back to the control center.

"Uh, no," he muttered to himself, the cursor still blinking at him, in sync with his heartbeat.

"Let's go check on the patrol units."

Ben rolled the chair back to the mapping computer and looked at the location of the green dots perfectly scattered over the map. A few red dots shot across the map as shooting stars, quickly pursued by a nearby officer.

Davis watched the screens for first ten minutes of Ben's lunch break. The radio was silent. The officers on patrol operated like a well-oiled machine. In boredom, his eyes shifted to the right. The cursor again matched his heartbeat. His eyes caught the form. It called to him.

"Where's he at?" he muttered to himself.

Davis rolled over to the computer and hovered his hands over the keyboard. He looked down, searching his soul for the motivation to type. He so wanted to enter that name. The boy in school who caused him so much turmoil as a pre-adolescent. Jacob Robert....J, he typed, but couldn't find the courage to type "a".

"What if they log these searches?" he thought to himself...but he already started.

J-A. He paused. Should he continue on? *C*, and heart fluttered with fear. Davis committed himself, starting the name. He couldn't stop now. In a fury, he typed the last two letters…O-B.

Just the first name, he muttered to himself, giving plausible deniability to a charge of looking up an old personal foe. Mere seconds later, the screen listed several people with Jacob as the first name. A few of the named stuck out, being highlighted in red. He clicked on the first red report, but no present location data pinged the map. The next red name, and he also struck out on real time location tracking.

He kept reading the names down in a row. *Pearson, Pearly, Ritter, Robert.* The name stuck out and flashbacks of the school bully danced in his memories. He stared at the screen, mesmerized by the name, but still carrying a petty grudge. He clicked the name, and a report displayed on the screen. Davis read the address, clicked on the Facebook tab to see some current photos and status updates, and he looked at the current car. The old school bully drove an old beater; something from the stone ages of the 2010s. Davis smirked to himself, in pride over achieving more than the old bully.

Davis clicked on the button to show a feed from his car's dash cam. The feed showed up, and it was driving down the road, a little too fast. The thought occurred to him to ping the speeding car to a nearby patrol officer.

How would I explain I knew he was speeding? He thought to himself, but remembered an officer would catch him automatically if the bully drove too close to the cruiser at the high speed. Davis smiled at the prospect of his old enemy getting a speeding ticket, but he fantasied of being on that stop. He pushed the other button on the monitor to look at the driver facing camera to see the old jerk singing to himself while cruising down the road.

Just then he heard the door cracking open, and he quickly hit the close button displaying the list of people with Jacob in their name and he hit a button on a random red listing.

"Looking at them girlfriends?" Ben laughed.

"Hah," Davis said with a hidden smile of terror, "Nope, just seeing if any of these warrants are on the road."

Davis was safe from his snooping for now.

IV – A Glitch In The Matrix

Douglass gathered his belongings for his first solo ride in the family car. His typically scattered brain checked off everything he needed.

"Do you have your wallet?"

"Yes, mom!" Douglas yelled as the door closed behind him.

Usually his excitement might cause him to forget simple necessities, but a feeling of maturity still lay lofty over his sixteen-year-old mind while he excitedly prepared for his first solo trip to his grandparents' house. Douglas was meticulous about all the rules of the road and smiled as he opened the driver's door to scoot into the seat for his maiden voyage. He cranked up the tunes and cautiously looked all around before pulling into traffic and heading down the road.

Davis perched on the edge of town in his patrol car, occasionally popping jokes over the radio to Taylor and Masters, his two best friends on the force. Six months since his first day and he was now flying solo, helping to take down the criminals in San Bernardino county. His computer alerted him to a dot moving toward him. The GPS relay flagged the moving vehicle, though the radar didn't agree the car was speeding. The lights went on and Davis pulled out behind the car.

"Masters, can you look up the car I'm tailing? Radar didn't show speeding, but the GPS flagged him for a traffic stop."

"Stand by."

"I'm on the way, Davis," Taylor informed over the radio.

The red Kia pulled over onto the shoulder of the road. Davis saw the figure of the person shuffling things around in the seat.

"He's doing something in the car. Do we have a visual?"

Masters clicked on the car and pushed the button for the driver facing dash cam. He saw the figure of the young man in the driver's seat fidgeting with something just below the visual line of the camera. A red button flashed, alerting him to a warrant. He clicked the button displaying a rap sheet reporting two decades of violent crimes. Another warning displayed on the screen: PRESUMED ARMED AND DANGEROUS.

"Hold back, Davis! Wait for backup!" The elevated voice cracked the radio. "All units in the area, we have a hit on Douglas Lanza. He's wanted on several violent crimes. I am seeing reports for over twenty years of convictions! He's fiddling with something just under my view of the camera. It's possible he's preparing a weapon."

Still, Masters looked at the mugshot and the kid who was in the car. There were certain similarities, but the boy struggling in the car appeared younger than the mugshots, or maybe it was the poor lighting as dusk crept into the windows of the stopped car. He thought about the possibilities of the records being wrong, or anti-aging surgery. Still, protocol said to take the subject into custody and sort out the details later.

Taylor rolled up right behind Davis, adding to the cover. The two officers concealed themselves behind the cars, Taylor unpacking his service rifle. Sounds of sirens filled the air as officers created a perimeter around the road. Taylor grabbed the receiver for the loudspeaker.

"DOUGLAS LANZA. WE KNOW WHO YOU ARE. PUT YOUR HANDS OUT THE WINDOW."

Inside the car, the sixteen-year-old boy froze in fear. He stumbled for his phone, but the sweat on his hands lubricated the device, sliding it out of his hands. He ducked down below the view of the window.

"PUT YOUR HANDS OUTSIDE THE WINDOW" the speaker again screamed. The windows opened, and the rifles pointed into the car from several directions. Taylor covered the rear of the car while another officer set up his cover perpendicular to the first two officers.

"Don't shoot!" screamed a high pitched, youthful voice.

"LET ME SEE THOSE HANDS!" the other officer barked at him.

The street flashed repeatedly with red and blue lights, creating a scene increasing with chaos.

Still holding his wallet where his newly minted driver's license irritatingly stuck, he reached both hands out the window.

"DROP IT!" the officer yelled.

Confused, Douglas squeezed tighter on the wallet. Bursts of tears started trickling down his face as he looked from officer to officer, all pointing guns at him. Fear paralyzed his every action as everyone yelled conflicting orders at him at the same time. In the confusion of commands, he didn't see the officer approach from the opposite direction. Douglas felt a sting and went limp, the wallet falling from his hand, making a dust cloud emanate from a thud where it hit the ground. He fell toward the wheel and the horn let off a scream.

"TASER DEPLOYED!" an officer yelled over the radio.

The officer slammed open the door and yanked the young boy out. For the first time, they saw this to be a mere kid, not old enough to be the perpetrator the records system suggested they were hunting. All the officers looked around at each other. Finally, Taylor picked up his radio.

"We need EMS and a sergeant immediately."

Davis picked up the wallet where it hit the ground and opened it up. The ID was stuck inside the clear sheath, but he could read the specifics.

Lanza, Douglas
Junior Drivers License

He noted the issue date and saw that Douglas had just passed his road test. Looking at the boy, tears streaming down his face as he sat on the ground outside the Kia, shivering. There was no mistaking the correct information on the license before him. The Roadmaster and department policy had led these officers to believe they hunted a dangerous criminal, and they hunted with full force. Davis closed the wallet and grabbed a tissue from his pocket.

"It's OK, son," he calmly said, reaching his hand out with the tissue.

Douglas sobbed, barely looking at the officer while reaching for the tissue. He wiped his face, wondering what had led to this state.

Lockdown

I – Lockdown

With a sudden crack, the townhouse momentarily reflected bright blue light from every corner before once again turning dark from the oncoming storm. The flash and crack startled Don back to his present reality. He rested on a blue corduroy chair placed squarely in front of the television: his usual place to stay since the company closed down the restaurant.

Don remained unmarried, turning his attention to his career, not as a mere line cook as some may precociously assume when casual American conversation demanded to know his occupation. He was, in fact, the general manager of his location, a long-time company employee. He started in high school as a line cook, but proved himself, seeing the opportunity to take management courses, paid for by the restaurant of course, as a fine alternative to college. Don did better than most of his peers, anyway. That was before.

Now nearly everyone he knew was out of work, wasting away in front of their televisions. A few of his friends were able to keep on working from home, if you could call it work. His best friend, Sam, complained that working from home was a distraction, especially after all the schools closed down. The balance to learn to work while perpetually distracted by the joys of family life is a daunting task, but at least Sam still had a paycheck coming in to ward off the mortgage bill.

Most of Don's friends used the opportunity to clean up their house. Don remembered the last days of freedom, had it only been a month? His restaurant was overrun with customers, to and fro preparing for a variety of choirs, stocking up on previously unsought items...who really needed that much toilet paper anyway? Other items were the paint to finally refresh that old room, or shelves, to organize the garage. Even Don participated in storing up materials for projects at home. The government-mandated break would certainly hurt the pocketbook, but at least he was out of excuses for the laundry list of household choirs. Like his friends and neighbors, however, cabin fever set in within about a week once he finished all the projects. Now he perched himself in front of the television with nothing to do. The thunder outside was a welcome change to the regular dreary clouds.

He looked back up, fixing his eyes on the television. The reporter had another update:

The virus is still spreading. It would appear from the continued spread that people are not maintaining the required social distancing, so the government has now issued a new order. Everyone is to remain indoors unless there is an emergency requiring you to leave your house. All essential employees will be given a license to leave their residence. Checkpoints will be established at key positions throughout the state. Do not leave your residence without a license. In the event of an emergency, call your local health department to receive a temporary license number. This new curfew will be in effect starting at 8:00 PM tonight.

Don reached for the newspaper. More news about the virus spreading in the big cities. The news reported few confirmed cases in Jefferson County, but the hospital sent all the infirm home to recover peacefully there. Still, the paper indicated Jefferson would be the test location for a new 'early warning' experimental protocol. The authorities opted to use Jefferson because the virus had not yet spread far into the community including a small city and several country towns. Lacking interest in the next sitcom rerun, he muted the television to focus on the new early warning system as presented in the newspaper press release:

The Mandrake Virus has been spreading across the United States, and other countries, at an unprecedented rate. Scientists around the globe have been working tirelessly to control the spread of the infection. Social distancing appears to be helping the spread in some cases, but nevertheless, the virus continues to spread. One key measure for control is to determine who has been infected by the virus. Jefferson County is pleased to be selected as the first test of a novel product that hopes to identify infected persons so better quarantine measures can be taken.

The new device is a ring which constantly measures your temperature and other vital signs. The Bluetooth connection to your device will connect with the app and notify you if your vital signs indicate you are likely to be infected with the Mandrake Virus. From the app, you can alert the authorities and they will deliver a home kit to prepare an official test.

Each resident's ring will be delivered directly to their house. The National Guard will help everyone set up the device, so please have your phone ready when they arrive at your door between 9:00 and 6:00 daily. In the event you are an essential employee, you will receive your ring at your place of work.

Don read the article a few times. He focused on the second and third paragraphs the most. He didn't need an education on the Mandrake Virus. Don, along with every other citizen of Jefferson County, and the state, and the country, and the world, had been receiving a daily crash course in the virus for two months now. It had surpassed education; it was now indoctrination.

A new device that always measures vitals. That might be useful information. Perhaps this would not be a bad thing. But Don caught a problem: He didn't have a smart phone. He knew for sure this thing would not connect to an app on his old landline. Yes, Don was not specifically anti-technology, but his formerly regular routine placed him at home, at work, or at church. All making a triangle of travel less that a few miles.

Not that he never traveled. When he did go on vacation, or to visit the folks, or on the short trips to just get out of town, he would borrow an extra phone from Sam. As simple as Don made his life, Sam's was equally not simple. He worked in technology. He knew about computers, and phones, and teleconferencing. Sam was a techno-guru. Perhaps the contrast between their two lifestyles was the reason they remained friends for so long. They could share their experiences with each other, giving one another just a taste of the differences between their worlds. For one day a week, every Friday, they would play cards, shoot the breeze, and laugh the day away. He had not seen Sam in a month since the first lockdown order. At least phone calls still worked, so he picked up his old cordless telephone and dialed Sam from memory.

"Hi Sam. Got a minute?"

"Sure, Don," his friend replied, "what's up?"

"I'm reading the newspaper about this new device they want to give out to everyone. Have you seen anything about it?"

"Just what was on the front page of the local news this morning," Sam said, leaning back in his chair.

"Well, it says here that it needs to connect to a phone app of some kind. What happens if I don't have a phone to connect to?"

"Yeah," Sam sighed, "I am not sure. I really do not want to put another app on my phone. Actually, company policy: I can't put anything on my phone anyway! The IT department for work needs to approve applications. I am worried about this thing, though. Apps can connect to the Internet. I wonder if this app shares data…I would expect it to if this is a test."

"Did you see anything about rejecting the test? Isn't there something in the law about requiring consent to take part in a study?" Don asked.

Sam had not thought about that, but his college ethics courses did indeed teach about human review boards, the application and consent forms, and the rest of the red tape needed for a human trial.

"That's a good question," he said inquisitively.

Don heard the click-clack of a keyboard as Sam hammered a question into a search engine. Don heard this sound before; he knew Sam was looking something up, so he let the air remain dead for a period of time, knowing his computerphile-on-call was likely reading an article.

"I found some info here," Sam finally voiced. He started to read.

> In light of the global pandemic, the Ring Relief Project, RRP, was granted emergency status to be deployed across Jefferson County. The project does not require consent because it is a non-invasive device that is worn on the finger. All citizens much comply with the order, exceptions will only be granted by special permit of the research office.

"And there is more here about whom to contact for more information and how the device works," Sam concluded.

"Is this a little weird to you?" Don asked, still trying to process this whole idea of being part of an experiment for which he did not want to participate.

"Yes, it is," Sam echoed his own concerns back, "I specifically wonder how it will work when I can't install their app on my phone."

"Or the fact that I do not have a phone to install an app on at all!" Don replied back.

"There is that. I guess the best you can do is ask whoever drops this thing off," Sam said, sounding distracted in the last part of the sentence.

Sam's office had just been invaded by his two kids, Mike and Alice, playing tag. Don heard the muffled laughs through the headset as they expended the pent-up energy on a rainy day. Don heard the laughing yells of 'I got you' and 'no you didn't'.

"Ha, ha, ha, sorry about that. The kids are taking a break from the assignments. It looks like I need to go do the dad thing for a while."

"Alight," Don said, "Great talking to you," and he hung up the phone. He studied the newspaper again, this time with a brick in the pit of his stomach, unable to shake of the malaise of being forced into a county-wide research project without a say.

II – The Ring

Don still work up at 6:00 AM. Being off work didn't change his sleep patterns, so he went through the morning news programs, getting the Mandrake Virus updates from around the globe. He was reminded that the East Village part of town in Jefferson County would be receiving the new devices starting today. The percolating coffee echoed through the kitchen–the aroma, enough to wake him up and start pouring a cup while the doomsayer on the television gave the latest numbers on infections and deaths. They were urged again to stay indoors and that anyone on the streets would be stopped and questioned.

This news was devastating a month ago, but Don, like the rest of his fellow citizens, grew numb to the new oppression. They were numb to the traffic stops, guard stations posted on the neighborhood exits, and numb to the loss of their jobs and other restrictions. The paper, the television, the empty streets experienced when someone was able to break away. It was like a zombie apocalypse without the zombies of course. But still, he had an eerie sense of the future for the first time in his life.

He looked up and down the kitchen, opened the door to the garage, even took inventory of the other rooms in his house. He searched high and low for something–anything to do. Anything that would keep him off the news for another hour. The harbingers of death beckoned him, and he longed to listen no more. He nevertheless sat down in his blue chair, the morning newscast still playing, and he clicked the off button on the remote.

The blackness of the television sucked all the noise out; silence filled the room. Don heard the furnace kick on. His ear turned to the faint taps of something in the walls. Those faint taps have always been there, like a water droplet of unknown source. Dead silence everywhere else. It was too quiet, and Don moved his eyes to and fro in the living room. He focused on the Thomas Kinkade hanging on the wall. He loved that old painting, reprint though it was. Don studied every detail from his chair. The style spoke to his love of the misty outdoors. This painting, The Forest Chapel, mixed his loves: the mountain, the stream, the autumn colors, and the church set in the woods. He wondered when he would be able to make it back to shake the hands of his fellow parishioners.

His eyes took another turn to the DVD rack next to the entertainment stand.

"Perhaps a movie," he thought, scanning the titles best he could from his chair. The intrigue propelled him closer to the rack. He scanned the titles, more clearly this time. He looked for a movie he had not seen in a while, finally settling on *I Am Legend*. Don slid the case out of the rack with a satisfying friction and popped open the box. He was off to forget about life for a short 101 minutes. Then he could find out what to do with the rest of the day.

Don just filled up his coffee cup and perched once again on the chair, watching the opening scene when a loud knock pierced the living room, followed abruptly by the doorbell.

"That's curious," he said aloud to himself, fidgeting for the pause button on the remote control. He finally found it, freezing the frame right when Will Smith was racing forward toward some deer in a desolate New York City.

The door pounded again, and he heard the muffled noises from outside, "This is the National Guard. Open up!"

Don set his coffee on the table en route to the door.

"Yes?" He said, swinging the door open.

"Mr. Donald Nelson?"

"Yes, sir. That is me."

"Our records indicate you live here alone. Is that correct?"

"Yes. That is correct."

"Is anyone else here?"

"No, just me."

"We are here to deliver your ring for the research project. I assume you have heard the news that Jefferson County is the testing ground for a new early-warning device researching a stop to the spread of the novel Mandrake Virus?"

"I have heard that, sir. I do have some questions about the project though."

"It is mandatory unless you have an exception from the research team. I have the forms if you think you qualify for such an exception."

"Oh. But that is not my question. I read this connects to a phone app? I called a friend of mine (he works in technology) to get some more information on this. The problem is, I don't have a phone. I don't mind this ring, but I don't know how it will work without a phone."

"We see a phone number here on your file, sir."

"Yes, that is a landline phone. You are welcome to call it and see for yourself."

The man at the door looked for something more to say. He was not certain how to proceed. The guard stared Don down, conquered by the one objection he was not trained to handle: someone who actually did not have a smartphone.

"Close your door, Mr. Nelson. I'll be right back," the guardsman ordered as he turned back. Don closed the door, but stood by the window as the junior officer and his senior commander were clearly baffled by a man who claimed to not have a cell phone.

The junior guard approached the door again. Don opened the door as he approached. Cool air breezed into the door giving Don a brief refreshment before the guard stepped up on his stoop again.

"Sir. We will need to ask you to step outside. We are required to search your house and car to be sure you do not have a cell phone. If you really do have one, you need to let me know, NOW."

Don let his anger show in his face for the first time during the exchange. He tempered his words, knowing that if it came to blows, he was outmatched both physically and legally. After what felt like an eternity, he finally spoke, "I do not have a cell phone. I object to a search. You say you have my number. I will bring you the phone." He did not budge from his position, his lips stiffening in his total defiance.

"Step outside, sir," the guard ordered again in a softer tone to defuse the tension in the conversation. "We will be quick, and it will be a non-destructive search. I will take you to the Sargent so you can speak with him."

Don knew he was losing the disagreement, "Let me grab my jacket, please."

Don left the door open and grabbed his jacket from the hook a few feet from the door. He also reached for his car keys on the adjacent hook.

"My car keys," he declared in resignation, suspending a set of keys between his forefinger and thumb like they, themselves, were contaminated.

"Give 'em to those guys," the guard pointed back to two other men, dressed head to tow in hazmat suits. They approached Don's house like they were trying to extract some alien, or maybe a meth lab out of the basement. One man had a scanner of sorts.

As they passed each other, the man with the free hand took the keys and held them tightly. They vanished into his house to do whatever they wanted to do. Don stopped looking back once they disappeared, and looked forward to the Sargent, who was standing at ease watching him.

"They are just scanning for cellular signals, son," the Sargent said when Don was brought up to an invisible six-foot distance between him and the guard leader. He had to chuckle at the arrogance of a twenty-something calling his graying head, 'son'.

"I never bothered to get a cell phone. Most of my life is lived within walking distance if I were inclined to walk," Don said to the man, "So how will this work, anyway?"

"We need to confirm you are telling the truth. If you are, you will be issued a receiver. It's basically a cell phone without a phone application. It'll give you the readouts of your vitals and connect you to emergency services. You'll need to keep it with you when you make your permitted restocking runs. It will automatically broadcast your permission to us, so you don't need to stop to check in anymore; the guard will usher you through."

"All clear, Sarge!" Another guard broken into their conversation after a sweep of the house and car. He walked closer to the two men, addressing Don this time, "I left the car keys on your table. I hope that is OK."

"Yes, thank you," Don replied with a hint of irritation.

The Sargent reached into the forward command vehicle for a little box, "Here is your device. We need to scan it in first. I need you to sign these papers."

Don grabbed a thick packet, still staring at the Sargent, "What if I do not like to sign documents without reading them?" he barked in defiance.

"Go ahead and read them. We have all day."

"And when I read them…what if I do not agree to what they say?"

The Sargent was now growing impatient for the first time, "Son, we are in a health crisis. You are a citizen of this county. You can sign those papers, or we can take you to jail. It's your choice."

The Sargent's eyes grew angry and his face blossomed into a rosy red. His hand slowly moved in the direction of a sidearm, but he tried not to make it obvious to Don, who was already fixed at his hand's intended target. Again, he was outmatched and out he knew it. His countenance surrendered.

"Let me just scan this over," he finally said, softening his tone.

The Sargent followed suit and calmed down himself, canceling his reach for the Beretta at his side. He forced a smile on his face when Don signed his name to the stack of papers.

"Please give me a copy of this, so I can read it in detail…it will be more exciting than watching the news," he snidely barked.

"No problem," he answered, "Johnson! Get me a copy of this!" He barked off to another officer who retrieved the papers and ran off with them.

The Sargent passed Don over to a technician who fitted him with a ring and synced it to the cellular device. On inspection, the device was a smartphone without a calling application. He could even download games and news applications on it and connect it to a wireless Internet line, if he had such a thing. He had his device, and now the stack of papers that were signed under duress, and he finally settled in to watch his movie.

III – The Device

The film only numbed Don's mind for a hundred minutes, and the rest of the day of nothing stared him down. He examined the papers that he was forced to sign under the coercion of the National Guard. It was legalese, a language Don wasn't trained to understand. He scanned the headings instead. They were all the usual headings found in privacy policies and terms of conditions, not that Don had ever taken the time to read one: Introduction, Changes to These Terms, Third Party Applications, User Guidelines, Warranty and Disclaimers, Indemnification, Mandatory Arbitration. Don flipped to a random section and went bug-eyed trying to read, let alone comprehend, the small print. The closely spaced capital letters forced his eyes into blurry blocks, like he had just awoken in the morning. He thought about calling his attorney friend, who helped the restaurant with legal matters. Was this thing even binding when signed at literal gunpoint?

Don's emotions whirred within him. He could still hear the muffled orders being barked by guards on the street. They enforced the lockdown, handed out rings, and set up cell phone apps for his fellow detainees. Don set the packet of papers down on the stand next to his chair and took the empty coffee cup to the kitchen for a refill. The cup made a thud noise when he set it on the counter, the thud echoing to the corners of his empty kitchen. He approached the window to peak out the blinds. Sure enough, the guards were still working down the street. His own encounter with them this morning still stirred in his mind. It was the most excitement he had in over a month, yet still one he had wished didn't occur. He reasoned his case would be a fringe longer duration between exits, but apparently, his neighbors rebelled in their own isolation. The blinds snapped back closed and Don turned the attention to the coffee pot, still half full of scalding Folgers coffee.

The coffee sloshed into his cup, the steam rising, causing a smooth whiff of aroma, melting away his thoughts. He headed again for the chair. He had nothing left to do in isolation. He flipped the news back on again and turned the doomsayer down to a minimal volume, grabbing the cellphone device the guardsman handed him. Don opened up the Mandrake Monitoring App. The device had only that single application sitting alone in the upper left corner on top of the dark green background photo sloppily topped with red letters, "THIS DEVICE IS THE PROPERTY OF THE UNITED STATES NATIONAL GUARD."

The government clearly assembled the Mandrake Monitoring App in haste. Aesthetic balance and design was callously absent from the screen which appeared to display real-time displays of Don's heart rate and body temperature. The readout on the top showed, "98.2°F" clearly his body temperature. A little blinking heart icon showed 67...65...68...65. The number fluctuated with holding his breath and standing up and sitting down. It became a momentary distraction to see how low or how high he could tease the number. Then, like a kid with a new toy, when the momentary high of acquisition fades, he set the phone down again and increased the television volume.

"More infections are blazing across the country. Hospitals are overwhelmed with patients, and doctors are running low on supplies," the news reporter announced.

Don stared at the screen for a moment. The scenes on display right now looked like the reports he saw last week on a different news channel. In fact, he was sure of it. He focused in on a sign posted on the equipment, realizing at once the error. The sign was posting a warning message of some kind, but he could not recognize the language. He knew at once the news report was recycling footage from a different hospital, not the regional hospital the newscast claimed to be reporting about.

Don grew irritated with the report, as if they intentionally stirred up his emotions. He reached for the remote and fumbled with the buttons for the off switch. He looked back down at the ring on his finger that he was compelled to wear by the soldiers on his street. He wasn't even allowed to leave…or was he?

Don picked up the phone-like device again and opened the app. He noticed a button on the bottom of the device, "REQUEST PERMISSION TO LEAVE." Don clicked on the button. He was greeted with another form:

"SELECT YOUR PURPOSE FOR THE OUTING," Don scanned the list: 'Grocery Store', 'Sick Family Member', 'Medical Emergency' were displayed on the screen. He selected the Grocery Store option.

"PLEASE LIST THE ITEMS YOU DEEM ESSENTIAL," and a text box appeared on the device with instructions, 'One item per line.'

Don rummaged through the cupboards looking for food supplies that were running low. He formulated a list: Noodles, Pasta Sauce, Eggs, Milk, Cheese, Toilet Paper, Soap, Coffee. He added a list of items and pressed the "SUBMIT" button. The app tarried for a minute, then the device blinked back a screen, "PERMISSION GRANTED." He was given further instructions about keeping the app open while he passed through the guard station, and to leave within the hour, or the permission would be revoked. Don busted with excitement at the prospect of leaving home.

IV – Freedom

Don wrote down his grocery list onto a piece of paper and left it lay on the kitchen counter. He prepared himself for the big event with the same detail he had prepared for his senior prom. He hastily showered and shaved, put on his best, fresh jeans and a polo shirt, he prissily coated his face with aftershave. Don felt as if he took for granted the freely coming and going prior to the lockdown. Even a trip to the grocery store was an event that stirred excitement. Once he perfected his grooming, he grabbed his shopping list, keys, and wallet, and headed for his car, device in hand.

The car door opened with the four usual bleeps, then the car was quiet. Don cranked the engine over, roaring it to a start. He waited just a moment while the revolutions stabilized, still high from his momentary freedom. Don pressed the brake pedal and pushed down on the e-brake before instinctively gearing the car for reverse. With a jerk, the car shifted into gear, and he backed out of his space.

Don pulled out of the designed parking lot for his line of townhouses and headed for the main road to the store. A guardsman waved him to stop, "We see you have your permission leave. This is just a reminder you will only have a single outing this week, and time is limited. We will be setting a two-hour limit. Your app will show you the time remaining. Head directly to the store and directly home," the guard repeated his required line with the enthusiasm of a postal working asking if your package has anything, "liquid, fragile, hazardous, or potentially dangerous." He would have repeated the line a hundred times per day if more people were able to leave for simple outings. Still, Don nodded in understanding and turned right onto the main, empty road, cranking the radio to receive maximum enjoyment for his outing.

He thought about the best way to drive to the store. The shortest route was usual and the most prudent, but today, he wanted to take a brief detour. The newscaster kept repeating how the hospitals were full of people, how the virus was spreading around the whole world. He wanted to take a casual drive by the regional hospital. His mind worked out a story to tell if he were stopped. It could have been illegal to make such a detour, but his mind raced with conflict induced by a reflection of days of similar, mind-numbing newscast. He worked out his route and jumped onto the highway to bypass town. Then he would take the exit just prior to the store, "to take the back road" he told himself. He was struck by the empty roads. The route he took so many times was empty.

"It is just like a zombie apocalypse," he said aloud to himself, checking the mirror for any sign of other cars on the road. Occasionally a car passed on the opposite side of the highway, but it was nothing like he had ever seen before, well, except maybe on Christmas.

Don took the intended exit that passed the hospital before feeding into a side road that led to the back entrance to the local grocer. He slowed down, glancing to the left, his eyes fixated on the nearly empty parking lot. He looked up just in time to see a light turn red. His brakes squealed, and the car came to the stop just after the line. He could have run the light. No other cars would have witnessed the event, and no traffic would have been in conflict. Still, he took the time to look at the hospital parking lot again.

"It's empty," he said to himself. He threw on the left turn signal and made a last minute detour to the hospital. The car hummed down the long entrance way to the lot, and he made the left-hand turn toward the emergency entrance. It, too, was empty, save for one person sitting in the waiting room. A solitary car took the nearest spot to the door, but the lot was otherwise empty. He sped past that lot to the employee lots. Even there, many fewer cars were in the lot than any day he had ever stopped by the hospital, which was quite frequent since he volunteered to visit hospice patients for church. It was clear the hospital was down to a skeleton crew, and not overrun with patients.

Don pointed his car back to the exit, fiddling with the radio, looking for a newscast. He became glued to the next report:

> Today begins the roll-out for the Ring Relief Project
> that promises to provide an early warning for possible
> infections with the novel Mandrake virus. Residents are
> reminded of the importance of participating in the
> study. We are asking everyone to stay indoors. The
> hospitals are already burdened, so please only seek
> medical attention if it is absolutely necessary. Once the

killed her flashlight and crawled deep into the weeds, lying as flat as she could on the ground.

Chapter 8:   Autopsy

Keene Saunders's body lay on a stainless-steel table. His once beautiful green eyes lay closed, never to see the world again. His wavy brown hair was slicked back, and his face was slack and peaceful. Even in death, Dr. Bob could tell Keene was a handsome man with boyish features. He had seen Keene a few times around town, usually protesting animal cruelty and giving people information as to the conditions of animals at meat plants and dairy farms. Dr. Bob had spoken with him on occasion and admired his passion, education, and vitality—made him wish he could go back to his early twenties and make better choices, do better things.

Dr. Bob stood beside Keene in a custom-made black lab coat. He clipped a small microphone onto his lapel, then plugged it into a recorder that he slipped deep into his pocket. He started a play list from an application on his smart phone. *Pennsylvania 6-5000* began to play over a small Bluetooth speaker that sat beside a tray of stainless-steel, medieval-looking tools. He put on blue exam gloves with a snap and pressed record.

"Keene Saunders, twenty-three-year-old adult male, five feet nine, which would be 175 centimeters. Weight, 187 pounds, so that's about 85 ... no ... 84.82 kilograms and some change, if my math is still good ... and since I consider myself a freakin' genius, it's good. Mr. Saunders, for unknown reasons, was in the large animal enclosure at the Josephine Animal Welfare Sanctuary, affectionately referred to as J.A.W.S.—where he was apparently attacked and killed by a rescued African lion

"I remember the good old days: steak and potatoes. Can you bake up a cubed potato in butter?"

"You know we can't serve butter here. We have butter flavored canola if that will work."

"I guess that will have to do."

She walked back to the kitchen, leaving him to his memories. He opened up his phone and read the screenshot he made from the article from this morning. He wondered how our world turned into what it became in the last fifteen years since The Counsel became the ruling class.

A plate containing real steak slide in front of him. He savored the smell. Perfectly browned onions slowed their sizzle, and the potatoes, covered in spices and artificial butter flavoring, emitted steam. He smiled ear to ear as his favorite meal titillated his taste buds.

"That is perfect." He said.

Julie looked down at him and nodded. "Need anything else?"

"Not right now. Thank you."

He savored each bite of his meal, thinking back to the times when he ate the meal a few times per week. Now they say eating too much meat will destroy the world. Now they want us to eat only the things that are approved with the Green Stamp. It is the only way to keep humans alive.

His thoughts raced with every memory until he stabbed the last bite with his fork. He admired the steak, unsure when his next meat credit would arrive. He still admired the golden-brown bite when Julie walked up.

"Do you wish we could eat this more?"

He caught her off guard, assuming he didn't see her.

"I try not to think about such things. I miss the old days. Maybe too much."

"What if it were possible to eat the old ways, to live the old ways?"

"It's not. You know the penalty for trying to eat classic food–you could get exiled from society."

"It almost might be worth it," he said, slowly inserting his last bite into his mouth.

"I long for freedom," he said, still chewing.

"So do I, but I need my business to survive."

William paid his bill and stepped out into the chilly evening. Thoughts raced through his mind and again a subconscious force pushed him toward Appleton. He walked down the street, removing his headphones as he approached the corner at fourth street. William looked all named Thor. Another lion, a female named Xena, who also resides in the enclosure, was not seen at the time the body was discovered. She is assumed to have been in her den. Weather was warm and dry on the night of the attack. Patient worked at the site."

Dr. Bob ran his blue fingers along Keene's neck to check the wounds, as he started to tap his foot to the bleating slur of the sliding trombone. His body slightly swayed from side to side, until the ending tap on the drum's cymbals signaled the song had ended. The rhythm and blues notes of the next tune gave a brassy entrance and Dr. Bob began his subtle dance again.

"The victim was attacked from the left posterolateral aspect, apparently suddenly or without opportunity for struggle. There are no defensive injuries, only punctures on the neck, transecting the right internal jugular vein and puncturing the right internal carotid artery. I can see a small laceration to the major vessel." Bob looked up at the X-rays an intern had taken and hung for him.

"X-rays confirm extensive soft tissue injury and fractures to the neck. At least it was quick. Patient probably didn't know what hit him." He shook his head to erase the awful image that had entered his mind.

"Claw marks are located on the left posterior and superior thorax, and left and right upper arm. Multiple sharp horizontal wounds, consistent with bites, present at the neck base. Other injuries and wounds on the body appear to have occurred postmortem." Dr. Bob looked up and down Keene's mauled flesh.

"There are postmortem bites around the legs and stomach, and he is missing two ribs." Dr. Bob looked at Keene's neck, then his stomach, then up at his head as the canned sound of a mute-muffled trombone playfully wailed, signaling the end to the tune.

"Postmortem damage also consists of puncture fractures of the skull and facial bones. Interesting … the marks on the victim's head are different than the marks on the neck and torso. The marks on the head look bigger and deeper. Maybe Xena got him first, and Thor tore him away. The divider gate was open, so it is possible."

The swinging beat of *In the Mood* danced across the speakers, and Dr. Bob felt his hips twist as he visualized jazz clubs, cigars, and scotch. He danced the *Charleston* over to his desk to get the files on Xena and Thor. He wagged his finger in the air as he had seen in the old black-and-white movies his mother loved. He then lowered his head and began reading the files, his body keeping rhythm with the music.

"…Thor, whose owner used pliers to
remove his teeth so that he could continue
to play with him, came to J.A.W.S. in a lot
of pain. He had to have multiple procedures
to fix the damage, due to his owner's desire
to make him 'safe' …"

"Jesus! What monster pulls out an animal's teeth like that? How about not having a lion if you don't like the love bites?" He skimmed for Xena's information.

"… Xena, rescued from a barn, and owned
by a traveling circus prior to that, was intact

64

around, listening for sounds as he slowly approached the staircase. He still saw the symbol on the door, and he looked around one last time before walking down the steps.

His heart raced as adrenaline consumed him. Butterflies danced in his stomach as he reached out his hand toward the door, and then withdrew it again. He reached out a second time, but fear gripped him. He withdrew his hand again and placed it in his pocket, staring at the door. Then he turned to walk up the steps.

He heard a slight crack and a creaking of an old hinge.

"Do you have something to tell me?"

William turned and looked at the stranger. He dressed well. A full suit and tie fit perfectly tailored to his body. His hair was clean and jelled perfectly in place. He looked like a person from the past, before everything was practical and regimented.

"Oh...uh...is this?"

He stammered over his words.

"Perhaps if I ask for an operational number, you might find your words?" The stranger said.

"Oh, uh, 101?"

The door opened wider, and the stranger stepped aside, motioning William inside.

"Quickly, please."

The door closed behind him, and warmth rescued him from the coolness of the evening. A glance around the room showed a small gathering of people scattered about, talking. A few sat quietly in extravagant chairs, reading books. Books he thought had long since been destroyed. The stranger led him past a few more people and into a room with a table. Fresh bread lay sliced on the table and he saw a yellow stick of what he thought might be butter sitting on the table.

"Is that butter? REAL butter?"

"Of course," he said, pulling out a chair in front of the table, motioning for William to sit down. "I'm Douglas, the host of this shop. Good thing you came. Tomorrow we are moving on."

Douglas reached out for a slice of bread and handed it to William.

"Please, help yourself to some butter. We make that bread from real flour, not the ACF you might be familiar with. In fact, there is nothing in there that isn't classic food. No science, just nature."

William held back the impulse to grab a handful of butter. He stuck a small amount on a knife and spread it over the bread, savoring every bite as he had done the steak earlier.

"This is a pirate store. We only operate a few hours at a time to prevent being found out by The Counsel. We know they are a little slow, so it becomes harder to gather evidence against us if we only stay for thirty-six hours. I take it this is your first time here?"

"Yes. I heard the broadcast during the Internet outage last night. I can say it stirred my soul."

"Of course. Now that you found us, we can tell you about the time and station of our next broadcast on this block. We don't write them down to not be discovered inadvertently. It will be on Wednesday at 20:04 on 101FM. We will announce our next store then."

"So, what's in the store?"

"We have kits for people to make their own food like the old days. We have recipes and ingredients. Did you already use your food credits for today?"

"I used them. At least breakfast and dinner. I rarely eat lunch, so I usually have a bunch of those credits in my account."

"When was the last time you used lunch credits, and how often do you use them?"

"I probably have lunch once a week. Tomorrow, in fact."

"Do you promise to skip lunch tomorrow if I process you a kit? We have ways to hiding the transaction until the following day. We trigger as a meal at a meal that is skipped so we don't draw attention."

"Of course, Douglas."

IV – Off Routine

Douglas passed off the kit and showed him the back door. William clutched his package tightly and made his way hastily to his house. Once inside, he slowly opened the package.

Happy birthday...to me. He voiced to himself.

The package included a small book of recipes. He flipped through looking at the titles: bread, tortillas, biscuits, pancakes. William set the book aside and saw a large bag full of an off-white powder. He opened it up and transported his soul back to his earlier life with the scent of flour. He smelled the familiar but forgotten odor of wheat flour. William saw a smaller bag labeled "powdered milk." Other basic ingredients rolled around the bottom of the package. A packing list suggested this and had all teeth and claws … very bad physical state with very serious malnutrition and suffers from osteoarthritis in the hips due to the time she spent inside a very small cage …"

"Okay, now I'm considering officially resigning from the human race."

He put the folder down then walked back to Keene, picking up a metal ruler.

"The bites around the face are consistent with large cat incisors and molars, canines absent. The length of the bite is twenty-eight centimeters wide. This fits Thor's defanged lion profile." Bob moved his ruler down to Keene's throat.

"The bites around the neck do show canine marks. They are 1.5 to 2 inches. These measurements are consistent with a much, much smaller cat. They do not fit Thor or Xena's profile. They are more consistent with that of a mountain lion, aka. cougar extraordinaire. Not a lion. Definitely not a defanged lion."

"The bite marks are not consistent. Plus, there was no evidence at the scene of a blood trail, or the patient being forcibly knocked down. This leads me to believe the actual attack did not take place in the enclosure, and the initial attack that led to the patient's death was not caused by an African lion, but a cougar."

The music slowed to *Moonlight Serenade*, visions of dreamy-eyed stares and romance filled the room. Bob stopped for a moment and reflected on a time in his past. He remembered his mom, young and beautiful, watching the old 1941 musical *Sun Valley Serenade*. He loved the classy way the women and men dressed, the shiny brass of the instruments, and the way the music made him feel like moving.

"Ah, my poor boy. You are never going to be able to hear life's beautiful music or fall in love."

It was now time to take intestine inventory. At this point, Bob had more questions than answers.

Chapter 9:   Ruben and Zane

Ruben held onto the leather-covered steering wheel as the F150 galloped its way down the unpaved, gravel back road. He had to go slow or risk damaging the new truck and pissing off Clay. Clay wasn't exactly the guy you wanted to have mad at you. He was part of a good-old-boy network that was still around. He had connections. He had money.

"Damn it, Ruben!" Zane yelled as his ass flew off the seat on a particularly big dip, and his head connected with the roof of the truck.

"Put your seatbelt on, dumbass." Ruben replied with no empathy in his voice.

Zane's sweaty, blond, chin-length hair flopped from one side of his leathery tan face to the other. He held an unlit cigarette between his teeth (no one smoked in any of the boss's vehicles). With his small, but toned arms—tattooed in sleeves of scantily clad, comic warrior women with big breasts, surrounded by skulls and fighting demons—Zane desperately held on to the grab handle.

"Seat belts are for pussies like you, Big R," he said, showing a mouth full of slightly yellowed teeth.

"You are such an asshole." Ruben said it jokingly but meant it as well. He didn't dislike Zane. He was trustworthy with secrets and loyal to a fault, but the kid had made enough stupid mistakes that he wouldn't mind if he decided to work somewhere else. Less hassle that way, but he was his half-brother, same dad ... different mom ... so he had a family obligation to look out for the little prick. But since they never lived together, he didn't feel that close to Zane.

"See anything yet, Zane?"

"No. What the hell are we looking for, anyway?"

"Anything that puts that hippy here. The sheriff showed up here, and Clay thinks there has to be a reason besides the complaints filed."

"You don't think we are going to go to jail for that stupid hippy, do you?"

"We didn't really do anything wrong. Kid did it to himself. Don't worry, the boss will take care of us."

"I don't know what you expect to see in the dark. This is stupid. Let's go to the bar."

"Boss said to take a look around. Besides, you're a real dumbass when you're drunk."

"You talking about that one chick again? Just drop it, man."

"Her name was Beth."

"Yeah, whatever man. She wanted it."

"You're a prick, Zane. You're lucky she didn't go to the cops."

"Like I said, she wanted it."

"She was too drunk to know what she wanted. You're playing with fire, you stupid bastard. I should have beaten your ass … just for being so stupid."

"Ha! You're such a diva."

"That's it. Stop messing around, asshole! When we get out of this truck—"

"Wait!" Zane pointed to the grass by the tall fence with the enthusiasm of a child seeing Disney World out the car window for the first time. "There was a light or something. A flash!" he said, his finger bouncing wildly in the direction of the fence with the motion of the truck.

Ruben stopped the truck, reached behind him, and pulled out a handheld spotlight. He aimed it in the general area Zane pointed to and followed the fence line slowly back and forth.

"See!" Zane tugged on Ruben's denim sleeve as the light reflected back like a castaway signaling for a plane.

"Yeah, I see it. Guess it's time to get to work. You're not useless after all, little bro." They both got out of the truck to investigate the light.

Chapter 10:   Don't Let There Be a Snake in the Grass

Mac lay perfectly still in the thick brush, watching a bright spotlight being shone from a truck. It followed a sweeping path, each time getting closer to where she was. She pressed herself as low as she could to the ground, her head resting sideways on her hands. Smells of sweet grass and weeds assaulted her nose.

I hope there's enough grass to cover me, she worried. Did they find my car? Are they looking for me? I should have hidden it better. The light crept closer … left … right … not far away now. Mac sucked in a breath and held it unconsciously as the light drew just a few feet from her face. She was frozen in fear as the bright beam paused, then quickly went away, back in the direction where she tripped, focusing on the bike. Two men exited the truck and walked towards it.

Tiny bugs, out in droves with the standing water from the rains, jumped in front of Mac's eyes as she tried to focus on the men through the grassy curtain. She felt microscopic teeth irritating her skin as the no-see-ums bit her. A drop of salty sweat dripped into her eye. She wanted to rub her eyes and scratch her skin, but she dare not move.

"It's right over here!"

If Mac's heart wasn't beating fast before, it was damn near sonic now. She wondered what would happen to her if she got caught. Mac shuddered. She didn't know what these two men were capable of and realized she might actually die out here.

As the men got closer, she recognized Ruben and Zane. Ruben was not a good guy, but he wasn't as bad as Zane. Zane was unpredictable. The grass crunched as they treaded through the weeds, not far from her.

"Holy crap, man. That's a sweet bike!" Zane whistled. Ruben looked down at the black Royal Enfield Thunderbird 350 that was lying on its side.

"Not an easy thing to pick up." Ruben commented. "Wonder if Keene put it on the ground, or if it fell."

"No wonder the sheriff came by."

"Shut up, Zane!"

"What? It's not like anyone is out here. All the hunters are gone."

"I said, shut up. Let's just grab it and get it somewhere." Ruben's voice seemed annoyed.

"Okay, okay. I'll come help get it vertical," said Zane. "What's your deal man?"

"Let's just move it as fast as we can ... get it out of sight." Ruben put the flashlight on the ground, and the two let out a groan as they stood the bike up.

"Hey, what's this … oil?" Zane rubbed his fingers together and smelled them. He bent towards the light.

"Dude! That's blood!" He rubbed his fingers in the grass.

Mac didn't dare lift her head. Fear grasped her, as she tried to turn slightly to get a better view, but the grass was too thick. If they come this way, can I outrun them to the car? I doubt it. She figured she was faster than Ruben but probably not Zane.

"What do you mean, blood? Here. Hold this." Zane took the bike from Ruben. Ruben grabbed the light, shining it around the bike.

"Man, I'm probably going to get AIDS or something." Zane whined.

"There's a little bit of blood. It is fresh, but we don't know if it was an animal." Ruben searched the surrounding area with his light.

"It probably wasn't. I mean, who would leave a free bike?" Zane spit in his hands and wiped them on his jeans.

Suddenly, a snake slithered through the grass and past Mac's face. She could smell its musky scent. She stifled a scream and backed up a fraction of an inch. Her clothes made a small rustle, and she froze.

"Hey, did you hear that?" Ruben pointed the light in Mac's direction.

"What? I didn't hear anything." Zane grunted as he started to push the bike through the field, towards the road.

"I heard something over there."

"Uh, a mouse, snake, frog? Pick one, pussy boy."

Mac's skin crawled with the image of the snake so close to her face. What if it crawls up my pants? What kind was it? The impulse to run was maddening. As much as she loved animals, she hated snakes. She tried to listen to Ruben and Zane to keep her mind off what was in the grass.

"Probably whatever animal cut itself on the bike is hiding."

"Shut up and help me get this to the truck. I got it stuck in a hole." Mac heard Zane shout, followed by more grunting and grass shifting.

"What are we going to do when we get it to the truck? I ain't lifting this."

"I think I have a board in the truck that we can use as a ramp."

Mac could hear the tailgate of the truck drop, followed by a board scraping against the bed. Sweat dripped down her face, and she could taste salt as she licked her lips. She lifted her head just a bit and caught sight of Ruben in the truck bed pulling on the handle bars as Zane was pushing the black bike up some boards.

"Whew!" she heard Zane's voice. "I think we found what we needed. Now let's get a beer."

"Yeah, let's go." Ruben agreed.

Mac waited until she heard doors close and the engine rev before she lifted her head. She caught sight of the truck rolling away. A sense of panic arose as she remembered her car, wondering if she hid it well enough. The truck turned around and headed the direction it came, and Mac breathed a sigh of relief. When she could no longer see any light, she jumped up and wildly swatted and swiped at the bugs that had found her, comically leaping in long strides out of the tall grass in hopes of not running into the snake.

With her light still in hand, Mac went back to the spot where Keene's motorcycle was just moments before. There was a large, flattened spot of grass, like a small crop circle, where it had been. She also noticed some singed grass. She imagined now was a good time to tell the sheriff. She would surely get in trouble for trespassing on the private road, but she didn't care. She had to do something. She couldn't just sit around and hope someone else cared enough to find out what actually happened to Keene.

Mac searched the immediate area but found nothing. Not even a dropped gum wrapper to remind the world Keene was here trying to make a difference in the lives of animals, she thought disappointedly. Mac felt deflated that there was nothing to show for her risking her life. She got out her phone and tried to pin the location so she could give it to the sheriff, but she had no signal. She took a mental note—as best as she could in the dark. She moved some rocks into a pile for a marker. She hoped she could bring the Sheriff out, and maybe he could bring out a team to search for forensic evidence ... if any of those *CSI* shows were accurate in any way.

After the rocks were in an acceptable pile, Mac dusted her hands off on her khakis and decided that was enough excitement for the day. The idea of running into Ruben or Zane again did not sound appealing. She followed the fence line back to her car as quickly as she could, then drove back to the rescue.

Chapter 11:   You What!?

It was nearly midnight when Mac walked into the trailer. Jenny was waiting at the small dinner table, a hot tea in hand.

"You went there, didn't you?" Jenny looked over her tea like a parent scolding a child. Steam rose and circled around her nose as she blew quietly at the hot liquid to cool it.

"Maybe."

"Well, I'm guessing you didn't get that bloody knee and scrapes from going to the store." Still in parent mode, Jenny eyed Mac's disheveled state with concern.

"I think Keene's motorcycle was there," Mac whispered, as if telling a government secret.

"What! Are you sure?" Jenny put the teacup down and sat up straight.

"Well, I didn't actually see it up close because it was so dark. But I'm pretty sure it was it was his bike. I tripped over it. That's how I got the scrapes. Next thing I know, Zane and Ruben showed up."

"Oh my God!" Jenny stood up and came closer to Mac. "Did they talk to you? What did they say?" Jenny's eyes looked frantic.

"What? No, they didn't talk to me. I hid." Mac gave Jenny a confused look. "Did you think I would ask for their help?"

Mac could see the furrow in Jenny's brow. "No. Of course not. I was just concerned." She pulled Mac in for a strong squeeze.

"I'm fine," Mac said, holding her. "They didn't see me. I was hiding in the grass." Jenny pulled back, looking horrified, as Mac continued telling her about the encounter.

"What are you going to do?" Jenny sat on the small loveseat in the trailer. It was a god-awful, rust color with faded flower patterns. Everything was donated at the sanctuary, which sometimes meant functional, but ugly.

"Call the sheriff, of course."

"Won't you get in trouble?" Jenny asked.

"I don't think that is the point. I saw Keene's bike."

"Right. I'm just trying to think this through. Were you looking to sneak onto Clay's property?"

"I wasn't ... oh, and when I was by the fence, some huge animal ran past me to catch a deer ... maybe it was a lion, or the lion in Keene's picture!"

"Mac, you can't even tell that there is a lion in that picture. Even if it was, that's definitely interesting, but you know as well as I do that it's perfectly legal to possess a lion in Texas. You just can't hunt them."

"Right, but maybe Clay *does* have African lion hunts. Maybe that is what Keene was trying to get proof of."

"Do you think that Clay would actually kill Keene over that? I know he was a pain in Clay's ass, but that's a little extreme. The worst Clay would get would be a fine."

"Maybe he knew something else. I wouldn't put it past that snake in the grass to be hiding something ... anything."

76

"Let me get this straight. You think you saw Keene's bike, but it's not there now. You think you saw a lion, but it was too dark to tell. Plus, why would Keene's bike be at the ranch and he be here?" Jenny gave Mac a look that made her doubt what she had witnessed.

"When you put it that way, it doesn't sound very convincing."

Jenny yawned. "Mac, it's well past midnight, and the morning shift starts at six. I think you saw something, but you should think about it. If you're about to tell the police you think Clay Jones has something to do with this, you had better make sure you have facts."

"Yeah, I see your point. The bike's already gone. A little sleep and a shower will give me time to think, clear my head."

"Agreed." Jenny got up from the table and started down the hall. "I will help you tomorrow."

Mac's mind was racing, but her body was exhausted. She followed Jenny down the small hallway and said goodnight. She walked past the bathroom, looking at the shower longingly, but not having the energy to bathe. Mac flumped down on the bed, boots extended over the edge. Tomorrow I will write all this down, get it straight, and call the sheriff. He'll help find out what happened. Mac fell asleep and dreamed of lions, and blood, and shadows.

Chapter 12:   Purr-fectly Annoying

While Mac slept past the morning sunrise, Sheriff Moore was at his desk looking at a domestic abuse file. "Damn it, Raymond."

"What, Boss?" Steve looked up from the file to see Deputy Allen staring at him. The deputy was twenty-seven years old and great at his job, though his boyish looks made him look about eighteen.

"Oh, sorry, Chris. I was talking to myself. That idiot Raymond Knight beat up Cynthia again. That man is a waste of space."

"She doesn't want to press charges again, Boss, but I have Veronica in there talking to her now. Hopefully, we can get her to follow through this time. If not, I'm afraid one day he's going to kill her."

A long, slender figure stepped in, cutting short the morning's discussion. Bob was in black pants with white pinstripes, which made him look even taller. He had a matching vest, black long sleeve shirt, and his cowboy boots. He reminded the sheriff of how the mayors dressed in Old West movies.

"Good morning, Bob. Have something for me?" the sheriff asked.

"Of course! This big cat attack is the most interesting thing to happen in this town for years, so it's top on my list."

"A man got attacked by an animal. We've had that before, Bob." The sheriff sat down and gestured to the pair of seats in front of his desk. "Have a seat."

"Sure, sure, but how many people have been found dead in a cage with a lion, but when the lion in the cage didn't kill him?"

"What are you talking about?" Deputy Allen asked. He got up from his desk and joined them with a perplexed looked that matched the sheriff's.

"Ah, gentlemen! I know it sounds pre-paw-sterous, but the evidence is purr-iceless!"

Bob's eyes glimmered in excitement at his own joke, and he leaned back in his chair, making the front legs hover above the ground.

"Being from the great state of Texas, I will admit to not seeing very many African lion attacks, and I am not an expert, but I'm damn good at cougar marks … the lion of Texas."

"This helps us how?" Sheriff Moore had a "get-to-the point" look.

"It helps you to know neither Thor nor Xena killed Keene. From what I can see, Thor just used him as a chew toy and light snack."

"You're saying a mountain lion killed Keene in the lion cage? That doesn't make any sense." Deputy Allen chuckled.

"Of course, it doesn't!"

"What? But you just said—" The sheriff held up a hand to the deputy.

"Let Bob finish this story before lunch."

Bob respectfully gave a slight bow with his hands pressed together, palms touching. "Namaste, Sheriff."

"I can't tell you where the mountain lion killed Keene. But I can tell you, if there wasn't a mountain lion in that cage, then someone moved the body." He slumped back into his chair, chin balanced on the contemplative temple his index finger made.

"How could there be a mountain lion in the cage?" Deputy Allen asked.

"Maybe it's the rabbit and the fence riddle," Bob replied nonchalantly.

"Don't say things like we know what the hell you are referring to, Bob." The sheriff complained. "What are you talking about?"

"There was this farmer, and a rabbit would come and eat his herbs, so the farmer built a fence around the garden. Well, the next day he comes out, and the rabbit is in the garden again. He looks all around and doesn't see where the rabbit got in."

"So how did he get in?" the deputy queried.

"He didn't." Bob paused a moment for affect. "The farmer had actually built the fence around the rabbit, trapping it inside."

"You're saying a mountain lion was trapped in the enclosure? Lived there without being noticed? Even Xena and Thor didn't know it was there?"

"It's possible. It's one explanation." Bob's matter of fact tone was light. "If the mountain lion wasn't already in there, that would suggest a more interesting theory that the body was moved."

"That would mean there was foul play," Sheriff Moore stated grimly. "Do you have anything else that can help us out, Bob?" Sheriff Moore knew this was good news for Mac, Xena, and Thor, but bad news if it meant someone was covering up a crime.

80

"Um, well, so far it's measurements. I have a ... forensic scientist ...friend." Bob air quoted, "friend." "Her name is Dr. Susan Vice. She is running reports for me on fibers and on the bites." Bob paused for a moment, looking past him and the deputy, to what could only be a memory of Dr. Vice.

A loud bang jolted Bob from his vision. "Snap out of it, Rome-o," the sheriff said, stapler still in hand on the desk. "What about the bites?"

"Yes, anyway, there are two different sizes of canines. Well, technically, one. The kill ones, the ones at the neck, are one and a half inches. The ones around the head are missing the canines, which must have been Thor's, since he's defanged. I don't think Xena got anywhere near the body. Lions are very possessive."

"You are basing this off an inch and a half of evidence?" Deputy Allen asked, then looked down as the sheriff shifted his gaze.

"Deputy, an inch is huge when it comes to teeth ... and sex. Also, the width of the bites was different. Once set—the lion's—is twenty-eight inches at the head and legs. The other set—the mountain lions—narrower, almost half as wide."

"DNA to confirm the difference?" The sheriff asked.

"DNA tests, I cannot rush. Take another day or two. I'm pulling favors and hopefully having dinner with the good doctor tonight. One man's catastrophe is another man's catnip, I always say. Well, I've never actually said it ... until now. Now, I think I will always say it. It's good, right?"

"Thanks Bob, you've been a great help."

"It's not only my job, it's my duty to find out what really happens to people. Dead men do tell tales, my friend. They usually have a lot to say."

"Let me know when you hear back about the DNA." The sheriff grabbed his jacket and stood.

"Right you are!" Bob hopped up and left with the dramatic long strides of the eccentric.

"Are you headed somewhere, Boss?" Deputy Allen asked.

"I have a few questions for Mac. She should have some information on the lions … and maybe a bit more about what Keene was doing."

"You need me?"

"No, but I want you to look at the animals Clay Jones has or had. Give me a list."

"Got it."

"Oh, and Chris."

"Yeah?"

"Call me on my cell. Let's keep this off the radio for now."

Deputy Allen nodded and went back to his desk to start his search while the sheriff headed for J.A.W.S.

Chapter 13:   Mornings Suck

Mac woke to loud knocking on the trailer door.

"Jenny. Get the door," she mumbled from underneath her pillow, but the knocking continued.

"Jenny!" Her loud call was only answered by silence followed by the sheriff's voice.

"Mac! It's Sheriff Moore. I have more questions."

Mac slowly opened one sleep-crusted eye and peered out from underneath her pillow. It was light out, which meant she was late for work. She groaned and rolled, rather than got out of bed. As she stood up, she winced at the pain in her leg. Dried blood crusted her pants around her wound and had stained the covers. She winced as she peeled the cloth away from her skin, which started it bleeding again. "Mac! Wake up!"

"Hold on!" she breathed. "Give me a sec."

Mac quickly took off her dirty clothes and pulled on a pair of sweats that had been draped over a chair for the last week or more. She pit-stopped in the bathroom and grabbed some make-up remover wipes to clean her face and anything not covered by the sweats. She ran a brush through her knotted hair and stepped back to look at herself. As she pulled a leaf from her hair, she told herself, "This will just have to do."

Another pound, pound, pound at the door.

"I'm coming, I'm coming. I just woke up; I'm late for work. I don't know why Jenny didn't wake—"

As she passed the table to open the door, at least one mystery was solved. A note sat against a coffee mug saying that Nancy had given Mac the day off. She reached for the aluminum door and opened it to find the sheriff, standing at a respectful distance at the bottom of the stairs. He was in full uniform.

"Nancy told me you were still in your trailer. I have a few …" There was a short pause as the sheriff took in the state Mac was in. "You okay? You look like hell."

"Rough night, but thanks for the flattery. This might be why you are single, Sheriff."

"Touché. Guessing you're not a morning person. Mind if I come in," he said, more like a statement than a question.

"Sure. Knock yourself out." Mac stood aside as the sheriff came in. He took off his hat when he entered the trailer. As he walked by, he said, "Oh, and it's eleven. Morning was a long time ago."

"Coffee, Sheriff?" Mac said as she gestured to the table.

"That would be great." He set his hat at the side of the table and watched her walk to an electric kettle and flip a switch.

"I hope instant coffee is okay."

"I actually prefer it." Sheriff watched Mac put a heaping spoonful of instant coffee in both cups. "Mac, you said Thor and Xena were defanged, right?"

"No, Thor, not Xena."

"We didn't find marks that matched Xena's profile. Is she tame?"

"Ha! No lion is ever tame. Don't let them fool you." The kettle clicked, indicating the water was boiling, and Mac poured the hot water over the coffee crystals,

84

releasing a strong, nutty aroma that smelled particularly good to her this morning.

"So ... all those TV shows with people with leopards as pets aren't real?"

"They are usually showing you very young cats. They get temperamental with age. A lot of lions that people buy as pets, end up at a canning plant in Colorado that sells their meat to gourmet chefs, or on a canned hunt."

"I had no idea people ate lions." The sheriff looked shocked.

"People eat everything. Sugar?"

"Black, thanks."

"As for not finding bites from Xena, lions get very possessive," Mac said, handing the sheriff his coffee.

"Yeah, I remember when you lured Thor away. He didn't like Xena getting to the milk bottle first."

"Him being the dominant lion, Xena won't get anything he has until he's done with it." Mac shuddered at the vision of Xena and Thor tugging on Keene's body. "Why do you ask?" She felt like she wasn't getting the whole story.

"Oh, just for clarification. This is our first lion attack."

"Did you ever find Keene's bike?" Mac blew on her coffee to cool it, then took a sip.

"No. We haven't. We have a description out on it, though, so hopefully it will turn up somewhere."

"Did you look at Clays? I mean, knowing Clay and Keene's past, and everything."

"I was going to take a look there myself. You were a stop on the way." The sheriff smiled at Mac.

"If it's there." Mac tried to word the question slyly, "would that suggest someone moved him? Could he have died on someone else's property, and maybe they moved him?" Mac stared at her hands. She could feel the sheriff's eyes upon her.

"Is there something you need to tell me, Mac?"

From his harsh tone, Mac quickly realized she had said too much, and wished she could take it back.

"I … um … well, last night … I just wanted to look around. Technically, I didn't go on his property … just around it." Mac drew a circle in the air with her fingers, as if the gesture would make it something other than trespassing and a stupid idea.

"You went to Clay's ranch, alone? When was this? Last night?!" The sheriff had put down his coffee. Mac realized social time was over.

"Mac, not only is that stupid; it's dangerous." Sheriff Moore stood and stared at her. "Why would you go there?"

"Keene left me a folder."

The sheriff's eyebrows raised. "And you were going to give me this folder—when?"

"I wasn't sure it was anything. The pictures are blurry. It's kinda like a diary, and it looks like Keene took a picture of a lion."

"A lion. A mountain lion?"

"No." Mac was getting frustrated. "African lion."

"Do you have mountain lions here?"

"What? Um, yes, one, but that's not the point." Mac was getting irritated.

"Where is the mountain lion kept? Near the African lions?"

"He's back further." Mac noticed the sheriff's eyes looked more serious. "He stays pretty hidden in his enclosure, but that isn't what I'm talking about. I'm talking about an African lion on Clay's ranch, which would be illegal to hunt." Mac felt satisfied she had gotten the message across.

"Can you get the folder, please." The sheriff placed his hands on the counter and spoke with an exasperated tone.

"Yeah, hold on." Mac ran to her room and dug the folder from the drawer. She brought it back to the sheriff.

"Clay is definitely not a man to be messed with." He looked up at Mac. "It wasn't very smart to go there alone."

"Right. Got it. No more Nancy Drew. More coffee, sheriff?" Mac tried to deflect the conversation and not focus on her trespassing.

"Nah. I'm good." The sheriff flipped through the pages slowly and read everything.

"See … see this picture right here?" Mac pointed at the blurred picture of the lion. "That is an African lion. See the mane here?" She traced her fingers, just like she did with Jenny.

"Mac, all I see here is evidence that Keene's been trespassing."

"Don't you want to know what I saw?" Mac stood opposite him, the counter in between them and her eyes wide.

Sheriff Moore sighed. "What did you see?"

"I saw Keene's bike. It was out by the fence, in some weeds." This seemed to perk the sheriff up.

"Are you sure it was his bike? Wasn't it dark?"

"I'm sure it was his bike. I tripped over it."

"That would explain your knee." Sheriff Moore pointed at a small blood stain forming on Mac's sweatpants.

Mac looked down and crossed her knees to hide the stain.

"Why didn't you call it in? I can get someone over there now." Sheriff Moore grabbed his cell phone.

"Wait, you can't … it's gone now."

"What do you mean, 'it's gone'?" That annoyed look returned to Sheriff Moore's face.

"Zane and Ruben came and took it."

Mac winced in a way that told the sheriff she knew what was coming.

"Zane and Ruben?! … Did they see you?"

"No. I was … hiding." The last word went up an octave, almost sounding like a question.

"Oh my God, Mac!" Sheriff Moore leaned back, hands falling to his sides in exhaustion.

"I'm fine! Nothing happened!"

"Okay." The sheriff bent over and pinched the bridge of his nose, his eyes shut tight. With a deep breath, he sat up and looked at Mac.

"Can you take me to the spot?" he asked.

88

"I think so." Mac felt like she could find the spot again. She was good at directions.

"Good. You go take care of that knee, and then we'll see if you can find the place you think the bike was."

"Aren't you going to look for the bike at Clay's? It may still be in Ruben's truck!" Mac started to get excited and exasperated.

"I'll get Deputy Allen to look at the truck, but with no warrant, the best he can do is wait for an excuse to examine the cab and the bed, which can be arranged."

"Why not get a warrant?"

"For now, Mac, just take me to the spot where you think the bike was."

"You don't believe me, do you?" Mac's face held a hurt expression.

"Let's just say, the more proof I have, the easier it is to get things done in this town." Mac went to get a Band-Aid as she heard the sheriff call in the story to Deputy Allen.

Chapter 14:   Bait and Switch?

Sitting in his patrol SUV, with a powdered donut in one hand and a 7-Eleven coffee in the other, Deputy Christopher Allen heard the call from the sheriff come in. He hurriedly shoved half a donut in his mouth and grabbed for the mic.

"Yesh, boss?" he mumbled into his radio. Powder from the donut coated his lips, shirt, and pants.

"Hey, Mac says she saw Ruben and Zane with Keene's bike in the back of Ruben's white pickup truck. I want you to check that out, discreetly, while I see if there is enough physical evidence for a warrant."

"Right, oh, and I checked on the animals at Clay's place," the deputy continued without waiting for an answer. "Aside from the usual like deer and turkey, there's gazelles, wildebeest, buffalos, including white buffalo, emus, ostrich, zebus—which is some kind of South Asian Ox ... basically a cow—and zebras. God knows why you'd want to shoot some of these. Of course, there are the cougars; they aren't protected in Texas, so they can be shot at any time."

"Right. Thanks for looking. Keep an eye out for Ruben or Zane."

As if God himself had heard the sheriff, Deputy Allen looked up to see Ruben's white truck cruising up the road in the opposite direction. It whipped past, Zane at the wheel, cigarette hanging from his mouth, and a passenger he could only assume was Ruben. He glanced at the radar and noted Zane was speeding. "With pleasure, boss. I'm on it," he said, as he let go of the talk button on the radio.

"Fifteen over the speed limit … hot damn," he told himself. He couldn't have asked for a more convenient reason to pull them over. A grin stretched across the deputy's face, so wide it would put the Grinch to shame.

Deputy Allen made a quick turn of the wheel. Dirt and rocks spewed from behind him as he slid the SUV back onto the road in a satisfying fishtail. He flipped the lights and siren on and sped up on the duo. The passenger, which he could definitely tell now was Ruben, and Zane seemed to exchange words as the truck pulled over. He pulled in behind them, got out of the car, and approached the already-rolled-down window. He could see a tarp covering a large object in the truck bed.

Deputy Allen walked to the window, he could see Zane's dirty handyman hands, with a cross tattooed on the middle finger of his right hand, resting on the wheel. As his face came into view, he could see Zane grinning, a cigarette dangling from his mouth. He worn an old, black Led Zeppelin t-shirt. Ruben sat beside him in a blue-plaid work shirt and jeans. A serious look on his face quickly turned into a smile.

"Hello, Chrissy," Ruben said, across Zane. "Nice day, isn't it?" He tipped a ball cap with the Big Bear Ranch on it, at him.

The deputy glared at Ruben.

"This isn't high school. It's Deputy Allen to you." He turned his focus to Zane. "Going a bit fast there, weren't ya?"

"Oh, really? I wasn't aware." His pleasantry was delivered dripping with false sincerity.

"Fifteen over. That's reckless driving." Allen peered over reflective sunglasses with a look of "I gotcha".

"Well—Deputy Chrissy," Ruben broke in. Zane snorted at the name reference. "Clay is having trouble with transferring an oryx. Of course, when he calls, we come running. Know what I mean? He being the boss and all."

"Still gotta follow the rules. Oh, and I noticed you have a tail light out. I'm going to have a look around if you don't mind. Wouldn't want you driving around without a tail light."

"Tail light … huh," Ruben's smile faltered. "I'm pretty sure they're all fine. If you're going to write a ticket, just do it, we need to get to the ranch … matter of safety."

The pleasantries had disappeared. The deputy felt his guard go up. "Yeah, let me just take a look at that light, and I will get you that ticket." He slowly walked behind the truck and saw part of a tire sticking out from under the tarp.

"What'cha got in the back here, Zane?"

Ruben leaned out the window. "That's a bike we found on the property."

"I wasn't talking to you, Ruben. I was talking to the driver."

"Yep, that's what it is." Zane called out.

"Well, I like motorcycles. I'm just going to take a peek here …" The deputy heard the driver's door open and drew his pistol.

"Hey, relax!" Zane exclaimed. "Hold up there, Deputy Dog. I was just getting out to help."

"Just stay there, Zane. I don't need your help." Deputy Allen lowered his gun and holstered it, but kept an eye on Zane, who stood there with his arms raised and a goofy smile spread across his face, unlit cigarette pinched between his teeth.

Allen reached over with his free hand and yanked the cover away. Underneath was a beat-up dirt bike, definitely not an Enfield.

"What do you think, Deputy?" He was startled to see Ruben opposite him with his arms folded on the side of the truck bed. "Think I can get her working again?"

The deputy paused. Not the Enfield, but something is going on.

"This registered to you?" He looked at Zane and Ruben.

Zane seemed to be taken aback by the question, but Ruben quickly jumped in. "Found it up on the property."

"How about I check the VIN for you?" Deputy Allen pushed back the tarp more, in order to see the numbers on the steering neck. He wrote the number down on a small note pad and pen he kept in his pocket. "You boys can wait here while I run the numbers for you, make sure it's not stolen." Allen walked back to the car slowly, making Ruben and Zane wait, for being smart asses.

"Don't mind if I reach into my pocket for a light to my cancer stick?" Zane called out. "Try not to shoot me!" Zane lowered his arms and fished through his pockets.

The deputy didn't reply. Instead, he called in the VIN, picked up the other half of the donut, then sipped his lukewarm coffee. The response from the station only took minutes, but he took his time. He watched Zane and Ruben exchange glances then stare at him with impatient looks.

After ten minutes, Allen got out of his SUV and walked towards Zane.

"Let's say we forget about the ticket, Deputy," Ruben said from the other side of the truck. "It was a slipup. Just trying to get back to work. You understand, right? Besides, we both know Judge Calahan will throw it out … him and Clay being old hunting pals."

"Don't threaten me with your bro network," Deputy Allen said, looking at Ruben. "I don't give a damn." Zane snickered at the profanity. Ruben stared in to the deputy's eyes. "One day you," he said pointing, "… or your sidekick, or your boss are going to make a mistake, and I'm going to be there."

Allen pointed at Zane. "You're lucky I'm in a good mood, Zane. I am going to give you a verbal warning."

"Oh, *most* gracious." Zane said in a sardonic tone.

"Oh, and fix that taillight," Allen said.

"There's nothing wrong with the lights." Ruben said, opening the passenger door.

Allen pulled out his club and casually smashed it when he walked by. "It's broken."

"Goddammit! Chris!" Ruben yelled as he slammed the passenger side and went to assess the damage.

The deputy stopped and looked back at the pair. "Now get the hell out of here."

With that, Zane put his cigarette out on his shoe, flicked it into the back of the truck, then placed a new unlit cancer stick in his mouth as he hopped into the driver's seat.

"Have a nice day." Deputy Allen tipped his hat to Ruben, got into his SUV, and called Sheriff Moore.

94

Chapter 15:   Missing: One Hipster Bike

Mac stood outside Clay's fence as the sheriff poked and kicked at the tall grass.

"Does this look familiar?" Sheriff Moore asked, trying to keep the impatience out of his tone.

"It was dark. I'm not too sure how far I walked along the fence." Mac was looking for the rock pile she had made, beginning to panic, afraid that she wouldn't find the spot. She scanned the field, hand shielding her eyes from the glaring afternoon sun. The grass brushed at the leg of her sweats, just as it had only a few hours before. She suddenly remembered the snake and quickly looked down.

"You all right?" Sheriff Moore asked.

"I'm fine." Keep it together Mac, she told herself. Snakes don't usually come back ... usually. Mac looked around to find something familiar. "Oh, up there. I remember the hill," she said, pointing.

"Hop in." The sheriff opened the door for her, then got into his side of the cruiser and slowly drove them up the path. "Let me know when you see something familiar."

Mac noticed tire tracks in the grass at the same time the sheriff did.

"Looks like those tire tracks are leading off the road and close to the fence," the sheriff said as he pointed. He turned the SUV from the path and drove up to a large patch of worn-down grass. They both got out and walked to the flattened patch. Mac could see the rock pile she made.

"There!" Mac pointed. "I left a pile of rocks to mark the spot."

"Good thinking," the sheriff replied. They both walked up to the rocks.

"Something big had definitely lain here. Look here." The sheriff pointed to the round patch. "See how it's singed? That could have been caused by a hot tail pipe."

"See!" Mac gave the sheriff a smarmy look.

"I said it *could*." He tipped his sheriff's hat back on his head. "Doesn't mean it was."

He continued to circle while Mac stood stoically with her arm's crossed. She could hear the grass crunching under the sheriff's boots as he examined the area.

"There's a little bit of blood here. Maybe yours?" He pointed to her knee.

"It could be." Mac threw the sheriff's doubt back at him.

The sheriff's cell phone vibrated on his hip. As he answered it, he instinctively turned away from Mac for privacy. "Yeah? … uh huh … you sure? Doesn't make sense. Right … nothing we can do now. I don't have much here. Right." Steve put his phone back in his pocket.

"What? What is it?" The sheriff turned, and Mac was directly behind him, so close she could smell his sweat and the laundry soap on his clothes.

"Deputy Allen pulled Zane and Ruben over."

"Great!" Mac felt excitement. "Did he find the bike?"

"He found *a* bike," he said.

"Well," he said, standing up, "I think I need to get home." But Robert found he was having a little trouble walking.

"Funny," he said. "Two beers never did that before." He yawned.

"You gonna be OK to drive?" Juan asked.

"Yep. Just need a touch of fresh air."

The two men walked out together.

III – What Happened

Robert felt his head before his eyes registered the light in the room. His head pounded with extreme pain. He didn't move but slowly opened his eyes and softly rolling his head in slight directions, glancing up to the sun shining through the window.

"I'm late!" he immediately thought as he tried to shoot up, but the pain was too great and he collapsed back into the bed. The grunt echoed through the room as his eyes shifted around. He reached for the phone that usually sat on the wireless charger for the night, but it wasn't there.

He closed his eyes again and mustered the strength to sit up. Immediately, panic set into his mind. His room was a mess, appearing as if it were ransacked. The gold watch he displayed on the dresser was gone. He shot over to look for the cherished possession on the floor near the dresser, but it was gone. His heartbeat intensified as he looked over the entire room for any memory of the previous night.

The tones of the doorbell echoed suddenly through the house, followed by several loud knocks at the door. Robert forgot about his headache and went for the door. He looked down to see he still wore his casual wear. He walked out of his room and toward the living room just as the bell rang again. Once he entered the living room, he immediately noticed the hole in the wall where the television used to hang.

"What in the world?" he shouted out.

The door banged again. Robert reached out for the door and it unlocked in his presence. He opened the door to find two police officers standing on the porch.

"Robert Miller?" An officer asked.

"Yes. Um. I think someone robbed me." He stood at the door, dumbfounded.

"Sir, your company sent us over to do a welfare check. Your office hasn't heard from you in two days."

"Two days!" Robert yelled, "I went to the bar with Sam just last night! You can talk to him from work."

"We have, sir. He confirmed you were at the bar on Broadway, but that he left before you. He said you were talking to someone when he left."

Robert rubbed his head again. The headache rushed back to him, and he grunted in pain.

"Sir, do you need medical attention?"

"I...I don't know. I just woke up, and I have a terrible headache."

"When did you get back home?" The officer questioned.

"I don't remember. The last thing I remember, I got up to leave the bar, but I can't remember when I got home. I just got up right before you knocked on the door." Robert thought for a second. "Let me see if my car is here."

Robert walked to the garage with the officers behind him. As he approached the kitchen door, he noticed the door was already unlocked.

"That's strange," he said.

"What?"

"The door. It should be locked. It locks when I leave it, and unlocks when I approach it, but it's already unlocked."

"Stand back, sir."

The officer drew his service pistol and reached for the door. He counted out quietly, three–two–one, and he threw the door open, pointing the gun into the garage. The car was in the garage, but the hood and doors were open. The officer went in with his flashlight. He shined it at the block and noticed an engine in disarray.

"Are you working on your car?" He asked Robert.

"No. That is a brand-new car. It's in perfect condition."

"Well, it looks like someone harvested it for parts."

"What? NO! I love that car!" Robert screamed.

"Sir, we need to get you to the hospital and lock up your house. It appears to be a crime scene. And if the last thing you remember is leaving the bar after talking to a stranger, we want to get your blood checked out. I think they have robbed you, but this is a pretty comprehensive job."

Robert stood in disbelief. He covered his face with his hands, thinking of the prospect of his looted house and car.

"Fine. Can you call my phone? I can't seem to find it."

The officer dialed the phone, but it went straight to voicemail.

"Nothing," he said. "We can contact the cell phone provider to find out the last known location. In fact, we should probably do that for our investigation, anyway."

"Please do that."

The officers and Robert put on gloves and carefully looked through the house, indexing all the missing belongings. Robert had a few safes, all protected by his chip. They were emptied of spare cash and other valuable belongings. His computers and entertainment system were gone, and nearly everything else of value was missing.

"How did this happen?" Robert asked.

"Well, our techs will get to the bottom of it. We have the list of what's missing, so we will alert the local pawn shops and keep an eye out. Now let's see about a blood test."

"We have concluded our investigation, Robert. Sadly, we can't recover the money that came out of your accounts. Your chip and fingerprint authorized a secure transfer to an overseas bank. They are stonewalling our investigation. It looks like a shell just to steal money out of our jurisdiction."

"I already had all my accounts changed. The office is holding my money until this is all resolved. What about the belongings?"

"We recovered a few items. I have the watch. They pawned it, but using a fake name, so we have a dead end concerning the identity of the perpetrator. The television and some of the other things are still missing."

"How did this happen?"

The officer handed him the reports. A toxicology report was on top. The analyst circled a positive report for Gamma Hydroxybutric Acid. He looked at the numbers showing high levels.

"What's this substance that's circled?"

"That is a common date rape drug. In the past, we dealt with a lot of rapes owing to it, but there is a new crime in the wings and that is the substance used. Do you recognize this man?"

The officer held up a picture of a man. Robert looked at it and recognized Juan from the bar. His face went pale, realizing at once what happened. Juan ordered the second round of drinks and spiked him. He kept up the

project is rolled out, you can request leave permission
to restock essential items only one time per week.
Please use your time wisely and report any delays
inside your app. Thank you.

"Hospitals are burdened, huh?" Don said, making his left turn back onto the main street. He sped on down the street toward his side road, but did not quite make it there when a police car flashed his lights, signaling an order to stop. Don's heart rate shot up, and the adrenaline made him sweat as he stopped the car on the side of the road.

He sat for an eternity while the officer took his good old time exiting his patrol car. As the officer approached, Don placed his hands on the steering wheel, perfectly at ten and two, placing both hands within view of the officer.

"Where are you heading to, sir?" The officer grimaced.

"To the grocery store."

"Why were you in the hospital parking lot, then?"

Don had already put thought into this question, "I was taking a different route than I usually do and forgot which road it was. I pulled in there to park for a second and get my barrings."

"Do you have permission to be out?"

"Yes officer," Don started. He grabbed the phone-like device and opened the app, handing it to the policeman.

The officer took the device with gloved hands and examined the screen, noting the timer. His facial expression melted from the initial rude countenance to a softer, gentler tone. He handed the device back, "Sir, you are supposed to go strait to the store and strait home. I see from your information that this is not a direct route. Since this is the first day of this program, I will let you off with a warning. Next time, you will be ticketed for being out of a direct route. Do you understand?"

"Yes, sir." Don had his share of fighting with authority for the day. He did not want to risk a ticket by mouthing off or causing any other sort of trouble, so he resigned his position.

"I'll add fifteen minutes to your clock for this stop today, but I want you to go straight to the store and straight home from there. If you need gas, use one of the stations that will be directly on that route. Drive safely, sir."

"Thank you, I will." Don rolled up his window and put the car into gear.

Mac gave an intense, confused look, and felt her brow furrow. "I'm not following you."

"They had a dirt bike in the back of their truck. Said they found it on the property. An old dirt bike, not an Enfield."

"Wha—no, it was Keene's! I know it was. I didn't trip over a dirt bike."

"Are you sure?" The sheriff lowered his hat back down until it was touching his eyebrows. "You did say it was dark."

"Yeah, I'm pretty sure." She placed her hands on her hips and closed her eyes, trying to picture the night. All she could see was fuzz and darkness, and self-doubt started to creep in. "It doesn't make sense. None of this does."

"It was dark, Mac. I believe you were here, and I believe you saw Ruben and Zane pick up a bike, but it was probably the dirt bike."

"I know I saw the Enfield," Mac said. "Why would Zane and Ruben hide Keene's bike? They would have had to know I was here, but I'm positive they didn't see me. Or at least, I think they didn't."

"I'm going to take you back." The sheriff headed toward the car. Mac continued to stare at the grassy spot.

Maybe it wasn't his bike, she second guessed herself. *You know it was*, said a little voice in the back of her head. That voice that everyone has that tells you exactly the truth, like, "You should bring an umbrella today," or "Don't go on a date with that guy, he's a perv," or "He's lying to you." That voice everyone should listen to because it does rain, he is a perv, and he is lying. But people seem to reason the voice away as needless worries, forgetting it was right, and make the same mistake the next time it talks ... which is exactly what Mac did.

I felt so sure last night, she pondered. Of course, my adrenaline had been pumping after running from the big cat and hiding from Ruben and Zane. A wave of tiredness flooded her body as discouragement tugged at her, her memory became fogged with the new information, and the crystal-clear image of the black Enfield blurred into a discarded dirt bike.

"Mac?" The sheriff held the SUV door open for her. Mac turned, tears streaming down her face.

"Keene's dead, there's no motorcycle, and who the hell knows why he was with Xena and Thor, BUT THEY DIDN'T DO IT!" Mac yelled the last words, as if making the world hear them would make them true.

"I don't have all the answers yet, Mac, but I will." The sheriff gestured to the door. "Time to get you back."

"What? Aren't you going to call out the forensic team or take a sample?"

"You watch too much TV, Mac. I don't have any reason to waste resources on what little proof I have that you saw Keene's bike." The sheriff gestured to the door again.

Mac stomped to the SUV and jumped in.

"I know what I saw," she said angrily, as she put her seatbelt. But as she clicked the metal latch and crossed her arms in a huff, she really didn't know.

The sheriff shut the door without adding a rebuttal. They drove in silence back to the sanctuary.

The oddness of the situation circled in his mind. Was he, or the whole population, being duped by a master plan to control them? Was the situation as bad as the doomsayers on the news were reporting? These thoughts echoed in his mind as he drove in silence to the grocery store.

V – Suspicions

Don pulled into his street with three minutes left on the app timer. He didn't rush in the ways they wanted him to. He was like a child, trotting alone without a care or curfew. They granted two hours and fifteen minutes, and he was not willing to give any of it back.

The guard waved him to a stop, "Do you live in this neighborhood?" He coldly asked.

"Yes, sir, I am just returning from leave."

The guard looked at an electronic device in his hand again, "Oh, I see. You took a few seconds to register. Thanks for being back on time, sir. I will grant you another leave in five days instead of seven for being on time."

The guardsman fiddled with his touch screen, inducing a sudden bleep, "OK, you're all set. Proceed directly home, please."

Don accelerated past him and turned the car into his townhouse parking lot. He clicked up the parking brake and took his time gathering the groceries. He casually strolled inside and breathed a resigned sigh of discomfort: he was back under house arrest. His crime? Living in Jefferson County.

The bags crinkled to a rest on the counter. Don shuffled through them, organizing the various food items into the cupboards. He slowed his pace to a crawl, knowing that nothing else awaited his time today, or even for the rest of the week. But still, being slow, he only took ten minutes putting everything away. He poured more coffee and slouched back into the chair in silence, sipping his cup in total boredom.

Don picked up the phone from beside the chair and dialed Sam again.

"Hey, what's up?" Sam said over the phone.

"I got the ring today, and went out into the world to buy some groceries," he said, a bored tone was detectable in his voice.

"Did you get your questions answered about not having a phone?" He asked.

"I did. The troops searched my house to make sure I wasn't lying, then they gave me a phone-like device to

Chapter 16:   Something Rotten This Way Comes

The sheriff dropped Mac back at her trailer. Mac, still feeling furious, pounded up the steps and slammed the trailer door as the sheriff drove off. Jenny jumped from her lunchtime nap on the couch, still wearing her boots and brown khaki uniform.

"Ugh! I'm so frustrated!" Mac waved her arms in exclamation and paced back and forth in the short space of the living room. From the time she left the field to the time she entered her trailer, she had played the previous night in her head over and over and decided she did see Keene's bike. Ruben and Zane must have seen or heard her and swapped out the bike. She didn't think they were that smart; well, maybe Ruben was.

"Jesus, Mac, what the hell?" Jenny moved the hair from her face. She was sitting up but slumped over, still trying to wake up.

"The sheriff!" Mac snarled, angrily pointing in the direction of now-departed sheriff. "That … man! I told him Ruben and Zane took Keene's bike, and he doesn't believe me!"

"What? Why did you tell him? You were going to leave this alone?" Jenny gave Mac an annoyed look that Mac ignored.

"I think there is something he isn't telling me." Mac dropped this nugget like it was yesterday's news and continued as she paced, talking faster and faster.

"He asked me about Thor and Xena's teeth. Why would he ask that? He also asked if we had any mountain lions."

"Why would he ask that?" Jenny seemed to be more awake to Mac now.

"So, I'm thinking, if Keene's bike was at Clay's, and Keene snuck onto Clay's property, then he could have gotten attacked there."

"What? Mac, why would you think that, and how would he get back here? You're not making any sense."

"The liability, Jenny! If Keene's death was accidental, or maybe they put him in the enclosure, what better way to throw off the trail then to blame it on another cat?" Mac felt like she was on to something.

Jenny lowered her head and grabbed her hair. "Oh man, oh man, oh man …"

Mac stopped. "What is it?"

"Well, first," Jenny raised her index finger. "you are suggesting murder. *Murder,* Mac. That's a little far-fetched, even for Clay Jones, don't you think? Second," Jenny's middle finger raised for effect. "Why would anyone move a dead body if it was an accident? And third, why switch out the bikes? You said it was dark; maybe you got it wrong."

"I know it was his bike! I just feel like there is something more here, Jenny. Keene wouldn't keep going back to Clay's without a reason."

"He had a reason—to mess with Clay's business." Jenny was getting up now. "Look, I love you, and I know this is hard, but what happened to Keene was an accident and nothing else. I'm tired and need some sleep."

"Sure, Jenny. You're probably right." Mac didn't think so, but she knew she needed to stop arguing.

carry with me. I think it is a phone, just without any way to make calls."

"Is it true that it always shows your heart rate and temperature?" Sam asked, intrigued by the new technology.

"Not on the screen all the time, but when I open up the program it tells me all that. It has…let's see…"

Don shifted the phone in his hand to retrieve the cellular device from his right pocket. With one hand, he opened up the app and looked at the screen. He continued, "It has temperature, heart rate, blood pressure. There is also a button on the bottom to request leave and another for emergency services."

"Interesting. I'll bet the app is sending all that data back to the people who are running the study. Like it or not, we have given up our rights. They are tracking our health data and there is nothing we can do about it."

"What do you mean, Sam?" Don asked.

Sam's voice jumped an octave, signaling to Don a deep passion in the topic they stumbled on.

"These apps, particularly those on cellular devices, collect all this data and send it back to a server run by the creator of the service. They can see everything, your heart rate, even when it changes if they set up system just right."

Don interrupted, "Aren't they just using this to see how the infection spreads? They don't really know who I am, do they?"

"Well," continued Sam, "'Anonymized' data, which they are claiming, means it doesn't have your specific name attached to it in their database, but such data is usually pretty easy to figure out who is who. For instance, they may not have your 'name' in the database, but I will bet when they set up the device, they know who has that specific device."

"Yes, I had to sign a bunch of papers when I got it," Don confirmed.

Sam continued more, like a five-year old expressing the painful details of a new toy, "They have the 'IMEI' number, which identifies the device. In this case, they know the number of the device they gave you. In my case, my phone carrier knows the device I have. But they also know your location. It will not be hard to figure out who lives at your house, which anyone accessing the database can figure out from the geolocation data stored in the database. It's easy enough to point to a place on the map, find the address, and search public and government records to find out who lives there!"

"So, they really do know who is who? Even though all the reports say that the data is not collecting any such information?"

"It really depends. What I am talking about here is what is possible, even easy, with this type of technology. What are they actually collecting? My guess is all that, but we can't know without seeing the database, and I will bet that is not public information."

Don allowed the conversation to go quiet for an uncomfortable amount of time as he processed everything Sam was telling him.

He finally found his words, "so, how 'bad' is this from a technology standpoint, Sam?"

"My guess? Pretty bad. This project could easily let every law enforcement and researcher know exactly who is where with real-time data. And the fact it can't be rejected is the worst of all. We have given up our rights and our privacy. We will have to wonder if we will ever get either of them back."

A sudden pounding at the door startled Don, "Someone is knocking on the door, Sam. Can you hold on?"

"Sure," he said.

Don approached the door, setting the phone on the shelf above his keys.

"Who is it?" He called back.

The muffled man yelled back, "National Guard. Open up!"

Don spun the deadbolt open and turned the knob, "Yes?"

"Donald Nelson?" the guardsman barked.

"Yes?"

"You need to come with me."

"Why, may I ask?" Don growled.

"Everything will be made clear, sir. But for now we are required to take you a quarantine tent," the guard was abrupt, but not rude.

"Why?" He insisted again.

"Sir, you will come willingly, or by force. Which will it be?"

A second guard slowly raised a rifle like a hunter not wanting to make any sudden moves upon spotting his quarry. Don observed the subtle action and shook his head in anger.

Don spoke a little more loudly, conscious of Sam on the phone within earshot, "Tell that fool to lower his gun and I'll come peacefully!"

The guardsman glanced behind him to the second soldier, motioning with his hands to lower the gun. The second troop complied and Don calmed his demeanor, speaking more softly this time.

"When will I hear what this is about?"

"Probably about ten minutes from now, maybe less. Will you come peacefully?"

"Yes," he growled again, resigning yet again to the tyrants at his door.

"Good. Please wash your hands and put this mask on."

Don backed away from the door, allowing the solider to come into his kitchen. He washed at the sink and put the mask on, once again being dragged out of his house by the National Guard.

VI – Quarantine

The guardsman led Don to an army truck that was waiting for him. The usual tan and green paint, distinctive of the now all-to-common military vehicles seen around town, covered the exposed metal of the truck, but the guard converted the top half of the vehicle into a cruel greenhouse. Opaque, green plastic wrapped tightly around a flimsy support structure. Strait ahead of him, another solider, in full suit, was holding open a plastic flap with one hand while reaching out to Don with the other. The man pulled Don up into the truck with him.

"Thank you for cooperating, Mr. Nelson," the man said, "Let's get you suited up, then we will answer all your questions."

Don peered around his surroundings, acquainting himself with the layout in the truck, which was clearly a medical unit. A solitary medical bed was bolted to the floor, the straps dangling onto the floor. A bench was on the far end of the truck with a bored solider leaning against a post, grasping an assault rifle like it was an obligation. Various screens for medical equipment were black.

"There is a headset there," the man in the suit yelled through his helmet, "and a suit. Put all that on, so we can talk more comfortably."

Don looked in the direction he was pointed, seeing a suit hanging up and a headset sitting there on a chair. Don picked up the headset, turning it over a few times, becoming acquainted with the various switches and knobs. He put the headset on and plugged the cable into the port, and turned on the transceiver.

"Testing. Can you hear me?"

"Yes," the man answered.

Don nodded in understanding and stepped into the containment suit. The man inspected for proper sealing of the suit and motioned at a chair, while he himself rolled up another chair to sit face to face.

"Sorry for the precaution, Mr. Nelson. My name is Doctor Douglas Schmidt."

"Fine, Dr. Schmidt. Can you tell me why I'm here?" Don barked.

"Absolutely. You were pulled over today while you were out, were you not?"

"That is correct," Don said.

"Well, the police officer who pulled you over is wearing the same ring you are. Shortly after your encounter, his sensors started going off, indicating that he probably has the Mandrake Virus. He is now in quarantine for further testing. Since you are one of the people who interacted with him, it is necessary to take the same precautions with you."

"So, how did you know I was pulled over anyway?"

"The device, in your case, and his phone, in his case, signaled that you two came into contact. This is a method we have called Contact Tracing. We let the software make the connections, and if there is a possible spread of the virus, we are dispatched to proactively quarantine everyone involved."

"So, it is not enough that I have to stay inside? Why do I need to be pulled out of my house?"

"Mr. Nelson, these are unprecedented times. We need to do everything we can to stop the spread of this virus."

"What about my rights? We still have a constitution, don't we?"

"Mr. Nelson, we are trying to save the world from a pandemic. The best chance we have is to isolate this virus early on. This is what our test is about," the doctor said, trying to be comforting, but Don was not as easily appeased.

"Doctor Schmidt, today I have been pulled out of my house twice by the National Guard and stopped unjustly by a police officer for the crime of driving to a grocery store while on a government-allowed leave. Now you are telling me that if that stupid police officer had not pulled me over, we wouldn't be here?" Don was furious, and he did not even attempt to hold back his anger.

The bored guardsman at the other end of the truck appeared to snap to attention. Don realized he could also hear what was being said through the headset. His fingers rested more precisely on his rifle, the sudden motion drawing Don's attention.

"Oh, and now I will have ANOTHER gun pointed at me!" he yelled even louder, pointing cruelly to the guard who was now snapped to attention with the firearm firmly held secure.

Dr. Schmidt turned around to see the solider now standing with his rifle half-raised.

"John, can you leave us alone, please?" The doctor asked in a calm voice.

"No, sir. You are not my commanding officer," the solider said sternly.

"Fine, you can stay. But can you sit back down?" The doctor pleaded.

John stood for a moment looking between the two of them, now all standing. He slowly backed up and sat back on the bench, though he kept a more rigid posture this time, keeping a keen eye on Don with his gun at the ready.

"Sorry, Don. Yes, this is unfortunate." the doctor took his own seat, leaving Don uncomfortable being the last man still standing. "Can you understand we are just trying to keep everyone safe?"

"Safe from what?" Don growled, "The only thing making me feel unsafe is all these guys with guns dragging me out of my house."

"Can you cooperate for another three weeks?"

"Three weeks of what?" Don insisted.

"Three weeks of testing, three weeks of quarantine. At least long enough that we will know you can't pass this on to anyone else," the doctor again pleaded.

"And if I refuse?" Don's rebellious side was getting the better of him. He had been pushed past his breaking point.

"Then we keep you longer," Doctor Schmidt said, staring into his eyes, "And we will add some criminal charges for interfering."

Don agreed to the three weeks of mandatory quarantine. He was isolated and tested for three weeks, and he never showed signs of illness, and the government papers he was forced to sign prevented him from ever telling anyone about his case.

Smart Control

I – The House

Dennis wrapped his hands around Julie's pregnant body, gently petting the bump. He slid his mouth past her ear and kissed her cheek.

"It's perfect, honey." Julie said, reaching up and holding his arms.

"Not quite. We just need to get the central air back up."

The new young family gleamed with excitement about their first house, blemishes and all. The market in Brawley, California, was about as good as it was anywhere, so they were lucky to have found a house that worked within their budget.

"It's perfect to me," she said, looking up into his brown eyes.

"Should we get to work?" Dennis asked, breaking the grip on her belly.

The couple went inside, opening up some windows to let the evening breeze cool down the house. The winter heat was bearable, but summer was around the corner. They had preparations to make for the baby, and also for fixing up the random odds and ends that come with a new, used house.

"The contractor will be here Tomorrow, so we'll have to plan for that. I'll handle that while you start the unpacking," the young man said.

The estimates for a new HVAC unit allowed a reduction in the price, but they still needed to pay for a new system. Dennis studied the paperwork, but the doorbell interrupted him sifting through the plans.

"Hello. I'm Johnson," the man said, standing at the door with his work uniform on.

"I've been expecting you," Dennis said, stepping aside and waving the man in.

Johnson looked at the unit and confirmed what the inspector said. The ducting in the house was fine after a cleaning, but the whole central air unit needed replacing. Johnson looked at the thermostat, nodding his head.

"We need to replace that, too."

Dennis looked at the thermostat, which looked fairly new.

"Really?" he said, still looking at it.

"Afraid so," Johnson said, "Another amazingly wasteful California regulation."

"Hmm," Dennis said, "even if the thing works?"

"Yep," the contractor started, "The recently enacted Title 24 code states that all new and updated HVAC systems require the installation of a wireless communication thermostat."

"So, a smart thermostat?"

"Yes, effectively. They want to be able to control your air temperature. Big Brother needs to know how warm you like your place, apparently!"

"Well, if we need to do that, let's go for it."

"Sure. It's already factored into the price. It should be on your quotes."

Dennis vaguely remembered seeing something about this, but thought it was just something for the paperwork. He looked it over again and confirmed it was there.

"No surprises," Johnson said. "We can start today if you're ready."

The rest of the day was a whirlwind of fury as the contractor pulled out pieces of the old system and added components for the new one. He finished up right around

5:00, saying his team would be by first thing to install the new system.

Dennis went into the nursery where Julie placed the finishing touches on the baby's room. In her excitement over the baby, she had neglected their own bedroom.

"Should I start on our bedroom?" he asked her, "That air mattress messed up my back... I can only image how you feel!"

Julie chuckled, "I'm sorry. I completely forgot about our room."

Dennis smiled back and left her to her thoughts. He started setting up the bed frame to assemble the bed. Two days in and the house was barely ready to live in.

Dennis was up early in the morning. He sat out on the back patio to watch the sunrise and take in the fresh air before the day got away from him.

"Howdy, neighbor!" he heard from the next house over.

Dennis startled to attention and looked over.

"Oh, hi," he said, "I didn't see you there."

"No problem," the man said, pouring coffee from a carafe into a cup. "I just stepped outside. Come on over. I have plenty more coffee, perfect for a morning like this."

Dennis got up and walked over, extending his hand in introduction.

"I'm Michael," the man said. "Welcome to the neighborhood."

"Thanks," Dennis said. "It seems pretty quiet here. I'm looking forward to it."

"It certainly is a nice place," Michael said, then changing the topic, "Is that new house of yours in good shape?"

Dennis detailed the general condition as well, except for the needed repairs to the central air. He also talked about the crazy new rule requiring the replacement of the thermostat with a new one that talked on the Internet.

"Those Internet connected things are trouble," Michael said. He seemed like a nice guy, but a suspicious one. "I know about that law, but you don't have to use the new thermostat. Just tell the contractor you want to keep hold of the old one, just in case. Once he leaves, you can install that one back on."

Dennis thought about it for a few seconds before responding.

"It's OK. I'll just let them install the one the code enforcement wants. It doesn't bother me."

"Suit yourself, but I warned you!" Michael chuckled, sipping his coffee again.

"What do you think is the worst that can happen if I keep that thing?"

"I don't want to think about the worst, but at the very least, they can see what temperature you like, and they might even have the power to control your settings."

"They couldn't really do that, could they?"

"Of course! It's Internet connected, and they can access the programming from online. If your app can change it, a hacker…or the power company can, too."

"I'm just not sure if it's a big deal. But, OK, I've been warned!" he said back.

The conversation paused for a moment as they both sipped on hot coffee. Dennis looked around the lawn, noticing that Michael had several older mowers and lawn equipment scatted about.

"You have some old machines lying around. Ever think to upgrade them?" he asked.

"Naw," Michael said, "the old gas engines work better." He paused, "Besides, if everything is running on the electricity, cars, chainsaws, weed whackers, our electric grid will be over-stressed, leading to brownouts. Diversity is the key!"

Dennis paused, thinking about what Michael said. He finally said, "Aren't they worse for the planet?"

"Depends on whom you ask," Michael said. "These things take batteries which require strip mining. The electricity might be from solar or from coal. But mowing my lawn every other week with a gallon of gasoline isn't going to wreck the planet nearly as much as one politician flying to New York for a shopping trip!"

"DENNIS!" Julie called out the door.

"That's my wife! I gotta go. Thanks for the coffee." Dennis chugged down the last bit of the coffee and set the cup down on the table. "Can we invite you over in a few days once we're settled in?"

"That would be nice. Thank you," Michael said.

Dennis walked back over and stepped in the back door.

"Sorry, I was meeting the neighbor."

"That's OK. I just wanted to tell you that the contractors are here. I opened up the doors for them."

Dennis went outside to talk to the contractors, but the discussion with Michael slipped his mind before they had changed out of the equipment and tossed the old thermostat. Dennis forgot about the old thermostat and was happy at the 7% the electric company had said they were saving by using the new smart device.

II – Heatwave

 The power's out again. I need to check on Billy."

Julie slid out of the covers and yawned to take in enough air for the push off the bed. She still wasn't sleeping the whole night after delivery. She walked out of the room, instinctively flipping the switch to the hallway light. But nothing happened. She opened the nursery door. The air purifier lay dead in the corner, starved of the juice it needed to keep the air consistent. The silence caught Julie's ear. She stopped for a moment, just looking at Billy, asleep in the crib. Finally, she tiptoed toward him.

His skin was soft and warm. Too warm, she thought. She dipped her hands into a bowl of water on the table and massaged it onto his skin. The baby stirred and whined, but kept sleeping. Julie placed her hand on his chest, feeling the rising and falling of the tiny chest muscles as he dreamed his dreams. Satisfied at his sleep, she walked out, closing the door behind her.

"The third time this week," she complained to Dennis.

"I know. And the forecast says it will just get hotter." He paused, "How's Billy?"

"He seems OK. A little warm, but for now he is fine. We need to keep it as cool as possible in there, though."

Dennis rolled off the bed and stretched. After catching his breath, he reached for the phone laying on the wireless charger on the nightstand. The weather forecast predicted even higher temperatures and a local notice warned of power outages.

"Look here, honey. The weather forecast says there are some power outages!" He joked.

"I noticed," Julie glibly replied.

Denis walked to the kitchen, still groggy from sleep.

As a ritual, he opened up the door and stepped out on the porch.

"Howdy, neighbor!" Michael called out, again sipping his coffee. A slight scent of exhaust sneaked past his nose and he became conscious of the faint noise of a generator.

"I got more fresh brew, if you're interested," he called out.

Dennis scratched his cheek and walked over to the deck. Michael already had an extra cup on the stand with the carafe of coffee, so Dennis just grabbed his cup and poured.

"Another day without power," he said, starting up the conversation.

"Yep. That's why I keep some generators and fuel handy. We keep pushing cars, tools, and everything to modern convenience to the already stressed electrical grid. Our present predicament is becoming the result!"

Michael's voice raised an octave as he talked about his favorite subject of preparation and the prophecy of the coming disasters. The two men already talked about preparing for harder times, stocking up on food, and being more self-reliant. For Michael, it was practice, but for Dennis, theory.

"We have been buying a few extra canned foods, but I just can't afford other things." Dennis said, admitting Michael had been right about being ready.

"It's gonna get worse," Michael said. "They're calling for record highs, up to 125 degrees. That means more people inside, more people cranking up the AC, and more stress on the grid."

Dennis could only nod in agreement. He paused, gathering his thoughts.

"How long do you think we'll be without power?"

Michael rubbed his chin, thinking about the issue.

"I would say it should be on in the next couple of hours, but expect some brownouts. Don't keep delicate electronics plugged in when you're not using them." He stopped for a moment, looking at the sky, deep in thought.

"How are you keeping your baby's room cool?" he asked.

"Right now, there isn't much we can do." Dennis said.

"I got something for ya."

Michael stood up and walked into the house. Dennis just sat still, glancing his eyes around looking at the various small engines and gas cans strewn across the lawn. He looked at the little generator pushing out power and the coffeepot still plugged into the portable energy source. Michael opened the door, breaking his concentration.

He sat down with a box in his hands.

"Let's see," he said, opening up the flaps.

He reached in and pulled out a black fan. He set it on the ground and kept digging around the box, finally extracting a cable.

"This is a battery powered fan. It should be able to run about five hours on the battery. Put a bowl of water behind it and should give a little cool air for the baby. You can just leave it plugged in, and it'll charge when the power is on, but run on battery if it goes out again. It's also safe from brownouts. Please, take it until you don't need it anymore."

Dennis picked it up, flipping it in various directions, nodding in satisfaction.

"Thank you," he said, smiling. "I think this will come in handy."

Dennis swigged down the rest of the coffee and headed back to the house.

"Honey," he called out once inside.

He headed toward the nursery. Julie rocked the baby on the chair in the corner, smiling when Dennis walked in.

"What's that?" she asked.

"Michael gave it to us for a while," he said, setting it on the table, positioning it toward the crib, "It's a fan that runs on battery, so it will keep the room cooler when the power goes out."

"Did he say, 'I told you so?'" she snickered.

"No. He's too laid back for that," Dennis said, but added, "but he reminded us why he likes planning ahead. No fan of our government's direction, that's for sure!"

They both let the silence fill the room, then a sudden noise emanated from the corner as the purifier choked back to life. Faint beeps emitted from various rooms of the house as random gizmos came roaring back to life with a fresh surge of power.

"Just like he said," Dennis whispered.

"Who?"

"Michael. He said the power would likely come back on, but we will probably have some rolling brownouts. He said to unplug everything that does not need plugged in to prevent possible surge damage."

They nodded to each other in agreement, then Michael stood up to roam the house to unplug the various non-essentials before making his way back to the nursery.

He sat again on the chair with his wife and watched as the light in the corner faded quickly and then flashed back to full brightness.

"I guess the brownouts begin," Dennis said.

He pulled out his phone and searched for local news. The weather reports confirmed Michael's forecast.

"We are expecting record highs today," he said.

He scrolled further. A report from the power company caught his eye. They reported on the power outage, reporting the blackout occurred from a series of burst transformers. After the first one went, a chain reaction of power re-routing overwhelmed the nearby transformers, causing a series of blown circuits. They blamed the increased usage of air conditioning as the primary cause.

The reports further called for the public to reduce their power usage. The power notice requires all electric cars and power tools to be unplugged immediately to save power for the air conditioning. Government requirements called for people to turn up their thermostats and not use excessive power. The power companies said they are going to invoke controls offered to them by Title 24.

Dennis read that last line and scratched his head. He knew he had about Title 24 before, but he couldn't place the conversation.

"Do you know anything about Title 24?" he finally asked.

"Not sure. What is it?" Julie answered.

"I remember something about it, but can't place what it is," he paused. "I'm going next door for a moment."

Dennis knocked on the front door to Michael's house, something he never did before. The door opened and Michael looked him up and down, also in shock that the conversation was in front.

"Never seen you here. What's up?"

"I was just reading the news, and the power company said something about Title 24. Do you know what that is?"

"Of course! That was our first conversation."

Michael unfolded the first conversation, being about the smart thermostat and that Title 24 required the contractor to install the device. The family forgot all about it because the thermostat became a convenience to them. Michael reminded the family that they could replace the thermostat legally. The couple thought the convenience was worth keeping the device.

Suddenly, a loud blaring noise interrupted their conversation. Both their phones emitted an emergency tone. They each rushed to silence the device, but they read the emergency broadcast notification.

Because of increasing temperatures and a record high, PG&E will throttle all smart thermostats in Brawley, California. Overriding the setting will be disabled. This allows us to keep the power grid stable during peak energy usage. Do not attempt to override the pre-selected temperature we have set your thermostat to. If you do not use a smart temperature control, please set your air conditioning unit to 85 degrees to prevent another blackout.

"There you have it, Dennis. They now have control of your thermostat."

III – Smart Control

Dennis opened his front door and walked straight to the thermostat. He looked at the setting for cooling and saw the number jump to 85 degrees. The house was already hot. The reading on the thermostat made him immediately feel the sweat balling up on his forehead. He felt the drop run down the side of his face, and he listened for the air conditioner. It didn't run. The current reading on the thermostat showed the air temperature right at 85.

"What was that alert?" Julie said, still holding Billy.

"It was the sound of Michael being right. The government just took control of our thermostat. They locked it at 85 degrees and said not to try changing it."

Julie's face twisted. "It's already hot in here. Can't we cool it down?"

"Not sure if there is much we can do right now," Dennis said, looking again at the thermostat, now seeing a lock icon on the display screen.

He pulled up the app to control the temperature on his phone. A notification popped up on the screen once the app opened.

Your power company has temporarily limited control over your temperature. Please do not attempt to override.

The app locked the temperature control. He showed the phone to Julie, and both of them just stared at the thermostat. The light in the room dimmed down, visualizing more stress on the power grid. The light snapped back to full power, and the numbers on the thermostat raised again. Now sporting 90 degrees, while the temperature in the house climbed above 85.

"This is ridiculous!" Julie screamed.

Billy fussed at the loud noise and settled back down.

"We need to get him cooled down," Julie whispered.

Dennis looked at his sweaty wife and nodded in agreement. He walked to the kitchen and started filling up jugs and bottles, putting them in the refrigerator. He filled up a few more pitchers and cups, creating an entire shelf of water.

"We'll keep some water cool, so we always have something cold to rub on him."

They both felt like the heat was increasing. Beads of sweat balled up on their foreheads, and they both grew thirsty enough to drink the cooling water.

The phone blazed another alert, and this disrupted Billy, causing him now to wake up and scream.

"I'll get him away from the phone," Julie said, heading back to the nursery.

Dennis drew the phone from his pocket and silenced the scream. He looked at the notification.

PG&E has declared an electricity emergency. We have locked all thermostats at 85 degrees, and we ask all citizens to reduce all power consumption. Do not charge your cars or power tools. Turn all thermostats to 85 degrees, do not run window unit air conditioners in any rooms you are not currently using. Take all steps to save power.

Dennis walked back over to the thermostat. The locked setting now read 100 degrees. The temperature in the house rose to 96.

Dennis went to the drawer with all the utility bills, shuffling through the pages to find the latest power bill. He looked up the phone number for customer service. The number rang, delivering him to a voice mailbox. Customer service was not available. The temperature continued to rise, and the air conditioning unit didn't start.

"Julie, the temperature keeps going up. The notice said the power company locked everyone's thermostats at 85 degrees, but ours currently reads 100. I tried to call the power company, but they aren't answering the phone."

The baby still fussed. Julie placed her hand on his head and a few other exposed body parts.

"I think he's getting hotter, Dennis."

He reached over and touched his skin, also seeing small beads of sweat on the baby.

"We have to cool him down. What if we run the car and sit in the air conditioning?" Dennis suggested, not sure if the AC in the car could keep up with 125 degrees desert heat.

Julie grabbed the dish of water and a cloth, gently dripping cool water over his face and arms. The heat kept rising, creating dangerous conditions in the house. Dennis opened the window, but the temperature outside was hotter, so he quickly shut the window again. He felt powerless over the elements.

"DING DONG," the doorbell called to through the house.

Dennis, still standing, checked the door, seeing Michael through the window. He opened up the door and welcomed the neighbor in.

"Wow, it's hot in here!" he declared.

"Yes, it is. They have locked our thermostat and last I saw, it was reading 100 degrees. I can't reach the power company."

The two men walked over to the thermostat and looked at the reading. It now read 110 degrees, with the temperature in the house climbing to over 106. Dennis noticed that the thermostat keeps raising the temperature once the air in the house reaches the setting by the power company.

"Did you try shutting down the power and turned it back on?"

Dennis liked the idea. They found the fuse box and shut the house down. After waiting about a minute, he turned the master switch back on. He heard the air conditioner kick on and sighed a brief puff of relief, but the system shut down again right away.

The thermostat number raised from 85 up and settled at 110 again, just above the air temperature.

"Michael, I have to get this placed cool. Our baby is starting to sweat, and it isn't safe in here."

"Well," Michael said, "My house is a cool 75. Let's just pack up and head over there."

Dennis nodded. "Michael, we need to move beyond this. What can I do in the long term?"

"Change that stupid thing out for something that isn't connected to the Internet!"

Dennis nodded some more. He left Michael in silence and walked to the nursery.

"Julie, gather what we need for a while. We are heading to Michael's house for the afternoon."

"Why?" she asked, slightly uneasy at taking her infant to the eccentric neighbor's house.

"Because his house is 75 degrees, and he is happy to help us out."

Julie silently packed up several things she would need and set Billy in the carrier. Dennis grabbed the travel bag while Julie grabbed the baby.

"We're ready, Michael." Dennis called out as they approached.

Michael opened the door for them and closed it behind them. They walked across the lawn and opened the door to Michael's house, which felt like a refrigerator compared to the blistering heat inside their own house. Michael pointed to a spot in the living room where Julie could set up a makeshift nursery and care for the baby.

The space was cleaner than Julie thought it would be based on her past conversations with Michael. She expected boxes of things everywhere, but it was a rather neat and clean place, albeit with a few shelves of random supplies.

"Get settled in, then me and Dennis are going to head to the hardware store."

Julie nodded and smiled at Michael for the first time.

"Thank you," she said, with more sincerity than she ever talked to him in the past.

"Where are we going?" Dennis asked.

"The hardware store. I'm gonna show you how to swap out that stupid smart thermostat so you can control the temperature in your home!"

iDNA

I – The Prosecution

The prosecutor stood up and glanced causally across the jury before making his opening remarks.

Persons of the Jury, throughout this trial, we will show scientific evidence that places the defendant, Bobby Wilson, at the scene of the murder of one Miss Jessie Vargus, on the night of the night of May 28th. We will show how he sought out her illegal services and killed her in cold blood, fleeing the scene of the crime, having taken without giving her the wages they agreed upon. We will show that he is a cold and calculated killer who deserves to spend the rest of his life behind bars.

The prosecutor for the state scanned the jury one last time, fixing his eyes on a few of the men, before sitting down in his seat again.

"Please give us your opening statement, counselor," Judge Todd said, directing his glance at the defense.

"Thank you, your honor." William Gates stood up, first compassionately glancing toward Mr. Wilson. He looked at the jury.

Ladies and gentlemen, it is quite impossible for Mr. Wilson to have committed the crimes he is being accused of in this courtroom. We have solid evidence from bank statements, witnesses, and toll booth charges that place Bobby in a completely different city while Miss Jessie Vargus was murdered. We will also show that Mr. Wilson is not a person who seeks such illegal services, and thus would not have had the opportunity or the motive to commit the crimes he is being accused of committing. Thank you.

Mr. Gates sat down and looked back up at the judge.

Judge Todd glanced at the jury and back at the prosecutor's podium. "Mr. Black, are your ready to present your case?"

"I am, your honor."

"You may begin."

Today, I want to tell you a sad story about the death of a fellow human being. This event occurred at a house rented as a short-term rental. A man and a woman consented to meet there for purposes that are known to be illegal. But what happened turned from controversial to cold-blooded murder. We believe that once the two people closed the door, a discovery occurred that made

the man lose control and murder the woman he brought
in there with him. It was not his intent, but it
happened.

Sadly, a hammer coincidentally lay on the floor beside
a table. Probably forgotten by a repair man fixing a
newly replaced window. That hammer became a
murder weapon used to brutally assault the woman.

Now, I am about to show you some disturbing
photographs. Photographs taken by the crime scene
investigators when they first arrived on the scene.
Please direct your attention to the screen.

Mr. Black picked up a clicker from his table and
pointed it toward the screen hanging on the wall. He
showed one picture of a dead body, mangled in the head.

This is the aftermath of the scene. You can see here the
poor woman who just wanted to make to money to eat,
is now deceased. Her head had been crushed in at
several points. She is almost unrecognizable.

Mr. Black pushed the button displaying another
picture. A few members of the jury forced themselves to
look at the screen. This photo was less brutal and more
instructive.

In this photo, you are looking at what is called a' blood
splatter' in the crime scene analysis world. You can see

three distinct lines. According to our investigator, whom you will hear from directly confirming his expert testimony, this means that Mr. Wilson swung the hammer into a raised position forcefully at least three times. So the victim was hit at least four times in the head.

Here is a report from the autopsy showing five distinct contact points between the hammer and the victim. Certainly within the three splatter patterns.

This is a horrible crime, but how do we know Mr. Wilson did the crime? As you know, we utilize science, and not speculation. We will soon show you evidence demonstrating Mr. Wilson to be the person who was in that room when the brutal murder took place.

Before I show you that evidence, however, I want to provide a motive. To start, you need to know something about Jessie Vargus. She is a transgender female. Now some of you may not agree with such a lifestyle, but is that really a cause to murder someone?

This poor woman was just trying to make enough money to eat. While the profession she chose to engage is illegal, murder is not the solution. We will demonstrate from social media posts here that Mr. Wilson hates transgender people.

"Objection, your honor!" Mr. Gates yelled as soon as the word 'hate' exited the mouth of the prosecutor. "It is mischaracterization to describe my client at hateful.

"Sustained," Judge Todd said. "Do not characterize the defendant."

Let me rephrase. It is clear from the social media posts that Mr. Wilson is an active member of a church that does not affirm the transgender lifestyle. This radicalization could easily lead him to the motive necessary to commit such a crime. To not embrace this lifestyle is to want to erase the lifestyle, so we have established a motive. It is our belief that he sought out the services of a prostitute, but upon finding she was transgender, he killed her out of disregard for her lifestyle.

Mr. Black stopped to scan the faces of the jury. He subtly nodded toward two people whom he thought looked sympathetic to his argument. He continued on.

The police recovered the hammer, used as the murder weapon, at the scene. The murderer wiped the hammer clean of blood or fingerprints, but the reconstruction of the crime scene with computer models shows that a hammer exactly like this was used in the murder. So we clearly see an attempt to hide aspects of the crime by cleaning the weapon.

Crime scene investigators found a print on the door lock. You can see that print on the screen now. Notice that it is a perfect match of prints we have on file for Mr. Wilson according to his biometric identification card. They also found DNA at the scene, also a perfect match for Mr. Wilson.

Mr. Black stopped again to let the jury take in the photos of the fingerprint and the DNA match.

Finally, we reached out to the property owner and discovered they have a camera in the room. Here is a relevant video.

The prosecutor played a video clip of a man and a woman walking into the room. The woman was clearly the victim, and the man looked perfectly at the camera, revealing a perfect match for Mr. Wilson.

The jury looked at the video clip of the man walking into the crime scene, and then they glanced at Mr. Wilson at his table. Many of them nodded their head in confirmation that the video showed them the man who was on trial.

Mr. Wilson looked back, scanning the faces. Nearly each person, having made eye contact, looked away from him. One man snarled at him, holding his eye contact menacingly. His heart dropped as the thought ran through his mind that the jury might declare him guilty. He almost thought himself guilty.

Persons of the jury, I have summarized our evidence. The defendant met Jessie Vargus and then turned to murder because of her lifestyle. We have the defendant at the scene with video evidence. Mr. Wilson's DNA and fingerprints were found at the scene, and we know he attends a church that does not agree with the lifestyle Jessie Vargus lived. We have location, evidence, and motive. Over the next few days, we will bring in expert witnesses to verify the evidence we have summarized to you today.

"Thank you, Mr. Black," Judge Todd said. "We will be adjourned for today. I want to remind the jury not to watch any coverage of this trial, and to be back at 8:00 tomorrow morning to hear from the expert witnesses."

II – Questions

 I am starting to think that I committed this crime, William! What's going on here?"

"Bobby, are you sure you didn't do this? I know I have your electronic records, but what they have is pretty compelling. I trust you when you say you didn't do it, but I am going to have a hard time convincing a jury of that."

Mr. Wilson looked down at the ground and sighed. "We talked about this evidence from discovery. Where did they get it? Any lead on that yet?"

"Not yet, Bobby, but my private investigator assures me he is close."

"Where did they get a single fingerprint that is perfect? Why did they only find one?" Mr. Wilson asked.

"That is a good question. I have never seen such a perfect print, and they only found that one print. These are good questions to ask the expert witness on cross examination. I'll ask him how frequently they find one print, and how frequently it matches the database perfectly. I still think they planted it and framed you."

"Why would someone what to frame me?"

"How active are you in the church? You are a visible member of the community. Is it possible you irritated someone with your mere existence or position?" William asked.

"Well, we protested the story hour at the library last month. I was there near the front of the protest. I *am* allowed to protest, right?"

"Legally, yes. But this world is getting divisive. If you are being targeted for that reason, it could be a compelling fact, but I am still not convinced it would be a good legal strategy to claim you are being targeted. It would actually solidify their claim that you hate the transgender population, even though I know you don't."

Bobby nodded along, still fuming at the attacks made against him. A ringing cell phone interrupted his thoughts. Both men reached for their pockets.

"Hello," William said, when his phone was the one that rang.

"Really? How soon can I get that? Great!" He hung up the phone.

"I have something we need to look at," William said, standing up.

Bobby followed him into his office, sitting at the chair opposite the lawyer's desk. William typed in some keys on the keyboard and sat back. A download was taking ten long seconds to finish, then he stretched his arms and leaned back into the computer screen. He transfixed his eyes on the screen, smiled, and nodded his head. William turned the screen toward Bobby and pushed play.

A video showed the same scene displayed on the brief clip in the courtroom. The door opened, and the murder victim walked into the room, followed by a man that clearly was not Mr. Wilson. The camera did not witness the crime, but it showed the exact scene showed in the court case, only with a different man.

Mr. Gates pushed the video to the side of the screen, snapping it into half the window. He opened the file on his computer with the same video clip from the courtroom and snapped it to the opposite side of the screen. He clicked them both to play them side by side. They were the same clip, but Bobby was not the man on the video.

"They swapped the face," Mr. Wilson said. "Who gave them this footage?"

William looked at his client. "That is exactly what I want to find out from the judge. But I want to know who this person is first. I need to make a call."

Bobby stood up and left the office, closing the door behind him.

"Is everyone ready to begin for the day?" Judge Todd asked, trading glances between both lawyers.

"We are, your honor," they both said, nearly in unison.

"Mr. Black, I believe you have some expert witness testimony."

"Yes, your honor. I will call to the stand Mr. Jason Whiteburn, the county fingerprint analyst."

Mr. Whiteburn sworn himself in at the stand and confirmed what Mr. Black said the prior day, that the single print was a perfect match for the biometric database. As he spoke, it was clear the jury tuned themselves into his analysis. He completed his analysis showing exactly why the presented print belonged to Mr. Wilson.

"Mr. Gates, you may cross-examine the witnesses."

"Thank you, your honor," Mr. Gates started, "Mr. Whiteburn, how long have you been a fingerprint analyst?"

"Twenty years, sir."

"So you are not new to this?"

"No."

"How many fingerprints do you think you have analyzed in your career?"

"Too many to count."

"Would you say more than ten thousand?"

"I would wager I could have looked at that many prints. You figure I look at a dozen prints a day at least. Over my years, it is possible to have looked at over fifty thousand."

"How common is it for you to find a single print at a crime scene?"

"I would say it's pretty rare. Criminals either leave behind several fingerprints, or they are wearing gloves and leave none."

"So one print in a room that a criminal has occupied is rare?"

"Correct, Mr. Gates."

"And how common is it to find a print that is in perfect condition as you testified that this print is?"

"Again, almost never. Usually prints are partials or smudges, and we can piece them together from fragments and collections."

"So this print is doubly rare. It is not common to find a single print, and it is not common to find a print that is nearly perfect?"

"Correct. This is the only case I can remember where this has happened."

"And you did not collect the print personally?"

"That is correct. I do not collect prints from the scene, I just analyze what I am given."

"So, Mr. Whiteburn, would be possible for someone to hand you a print that did not originate from the scene and say it was from the scene?"

"In theory, it is obviously possible, but we have the chain of custody for the print."

"And what is the chain of custody of this print? I did not see any photos in my discovery process that showed who collected the print or from where. Can you give me that information?"

"Sorry, I do not have that information. It should all be in the case files."

"Yes, sir, it should be, but it is not."

Mr. Gates stopped and let the silence hang in the courtroom while he scanned the jury. A few people were clearly in deep thought. Mr. Gates turned back to his table and picked up a paper.

"I have here, your honor, people of the jury, my discovery page on this fingerprint, and I am not seeing the details on its collection. I would like to move to have the print removed from the evidence."

"We will take a recess while I look over this paper more closely," Judge Todd said.

III – The Defense

Mr. Gates, you are prepared to provide your defense?"

"Yes, your honor."

Mr. Gates stood up from his table and addressed the jury.

Ladies and gentlemen of the jury, we have shown in our cross-examination that the evidence provided by the prosecutor has questionable origins and curious results. We will address our theory of that supposed evidence, but first, we want to bring to your attention records that place my client in a completely different city when someone committed this heinous crime. To be clear, it is tragic that someone had to lose their life, and we would not wish that on anyone, nor their family. But I will present clear evidence that my client was not in the city when this crime was committed. We will also show that he has no motive for this attack, and finally, we will present our theory on the evidence that has been presented.

Mr. Gates stepped back from the jury box and shuffled through some papers on his table.

How often is your bank wrong? Especially when you have gone back to ask them to double check their information? I would wager they are very right most of the time. Here is Mr. Wilson's actual calendar where you can see he has a business meeting scheduled in Atlanta, Georgia. Of course, a meeting on a calendar is not proof, so here are some emails exchanges.

Mr. Gates clicked through a screen of emails from before the date the of crime planning the meeting, the minutes of the meeting confirmed by the other company, and the email exchanges after the meeting. He suggested that a lot of people had to be lying to make up the idea that he killed anyone in a different city while in Atlanta.

"But meetings from a partner firm are not proof enough for some people, so here are some records from his bank."

Mr. Gates flipped through transaction records showing a national bank receipt for an ATM transaction in Atlanta. He also showed a video of Mr. Wilson at the ATM on location in Atlanta.

Here is a notarized document from the bank confirming that Mr. Wilson himself made the transaction in Atlanta, Georgia. Here is another when he deposited a sizable check into the bank branch in town the day of the murder. It is quite impossible for Mr. Wilson to have been killing anyone on the other side of the country only three hours after visiting a bank.

Mr. Gates put down the documents and addressed the jury.

"Ladies and gentlemen, do you hate people who disagree with you?"

He let his question uncomfortably hang in the air. He saw a few people on the jury joggle their head sideways before continuing.

The prosecutor has suggested that my client has a motive to murder someone because he attends a church that believes things about the Bible that have been believed for centuries. That is not hate, and that is certainly no motive for a person to kill another person for a disagreement. There is a section of our current society that suggests disagreeing with lifestyle choices means hate, but is it really hate? Maybe it is just a difference in opinion. As to the suggestion that Mr. Wilson would purchase the illegal service being sold by the victim, we searched high and low for any evidence that he might do such a thing. We did not find any, nor was the prosecutor able to give us any evidence. It all points to the fact that my client is not a person who would seek the illegal services in question.

He again paused, scanning the jury for evidence that they accepted his alternative theory to motivation. He again waited, making eye contact with several jurors.

"Now, we want to provide you with our theory for this 'scientific' evidence."

He picked up another piece of paper.

This is the text for a new law. It is a controversial law that passed on very narrow margins. It is the law that requires our new biometric identification cards. You know, the ones that require fingerprints, DNA samples, voice samples, and a retinal scan? This new ID has been rolling out on a lottery system and I have here the records from this identification project. You can see here that Mr. Wilson supplied the information as required by the law and now his private biomarkers are in a centralized government database. You all know that the privacy advocacy organizations warned that centralized databases mean top-down control, and access to information that could be used to plant evidence.

He waited for some reaction, and as he thought, a few of the jurors gave nods of concern.

We gained access to his information in the database and we found perfect DNA evidence and perfect fingerprint matches, both very rare to find. Tomorrow, you will hear from our expert witness how DNA evidence could be generated to a known standard. We already heard from cross-examination of Mr. Whiteburn that it is possible for fingerprint evidence to be planted. These points taken together suggest someone who wanted to plant evidence against a person needs only the information in that database. We believe that indeed, someone specifically targeted Mr. Wilson and used the new centralized database to plant evidence against him.

"Your honor, this is ridiculous!" Mr. Black yelled.

"Order in the court!"

Mr. Black sat back down and sighed.

"Apologies, your honor. I object to his line of questioning. The defense is claiming a huge conspiracy to defend a murderer!"

"Objection, your honor!" Mr. Gates yelled out, "He is again characterizing my client!"

"Both of you sit down!" Judge Todd yelled, hitting the gavel. "Again, do not characterize the defendant, Mr. Black. As to the other objection, I will allow this questioning to go on a little further. After all, there is some question about the fingerprint, which we have struck from the evidence."

The judge let the room draw silent again.

"Mr. Gates, you may continue your arguments."

"Thank you, your honor." Mr. Gates stopped to address the jury. "I have here a video that you already saw. Or at least you think you saw. I am about to show you more of the video. Video that my private investigator received directly from the owner of the house where the murder took place."

The attention turned to the screen where a video played. Jury members nodded, remembering the video, but the face was different. The face resembled a person not present in the courtroom, but it appeared to be the same video, including the timestamp.

You see, ladies and gentlemen, like the questionable fingerprints, this video raises more questions about my client's presence at the house in question on the night in question. Here are the two videos side by side. You can see they are identical save for the face. I know my copy comes from the owner of the house. But the prosecutor handed the one showing my client to me during our discovery phase. Tomorrow, you will hear from the owner of the house that my copy is genuine. In fact, mine is even longer and shows something curious.

Mr. Gates pressed the fast-forward button to show the video timestamp without anyone in the frame moving by rapidly. Then he slowed down to real time speed for the last thirty seconds that showed the same man wiping down the door lock before exiting the house.

You can see that our mystery man wipes down the lock before leaving. This is the same lock that the fingerprints, now struck from the record, were supposedly discovered. So, how did my client's perfect fingerprint get on a perfectly wiped down door lock when the last person on video accessing the house was not him? This does not make much sense to me. So we have a mystery fingerprint, DNA that we heard said, 'came from the defendant' and a door lock that has been wiped clean suddenly having a perfect fingerprint exactly matching the biometric identification database. Something seems fishy here. It was once said, "show me the man, I'll show you the crime." We have a way to show anyone guilty. Do we have enough control over the data to make sure this did not happen here?

Mr. Gates stopped and looked at the jury, making eye contact with the people he noted earlier seemed uncomfortable with the new identification.

IV – The Verdict

The jury shuffled into the meeting room, seating themselves randomly around the table. They looked at each other before one spoke up.

"Who will be the foreperson here?"

The group glanced eyes around the room, looking for any signs of movement.

"You can do it," a lady said, addressing the man who spoke.

"Does anyone else want the job?"

The only noise came from the buzzing institutional overhead lights.

"Alright, I will take care of this so we can move on. My name is John."

A few of them nodded at his name. A few others verbally expressed a hello.

"I guess the first thing we need to do is walk through the evidence and testimony. Does anything stand out to anyone?"

An older man in the corner spoke up first. "I'm not sure what in the world is going on in this case. How is it we saw two videos that looked the same with just a different person in it? Can we trust either of the videos?"

A younger man, probably just out of college, answered the question the older man asked. "This is pretty easy to do with the new AI models. If we just have a few pictures of a person, and it is pretty easy to put them on any video we want."

"So how do we know which one is the right one? Or if any are correct?" The old man looked at the younger man. "Oh, I'm Ben. What's your name, sir?"

"Johnny," the kid said, "Nice to meet you. I would say if any are correct, it's probably the longer video. The one that didn't show Mr. Wilson in it. But it's also possible to make a video that extends the shorter one. We would just need to trust which one the court gives us as real. John, what do you think?"

"Don't look at me. I'm a bricklayer. Does anyone one else have any idea about it?"

A woman with a scowl on her face chimed in, "I think the video that shows Mr. Wilson going into the place is real. The police would not give us a fake video. The private investigator who gave it to Mr. Wilson could have made it to make him look innocent. I am inclined to think he did it."

The room turned in near unison to Johnny. He saw everyone looking at him and felt compelled to answer. "It is certainly possible. AI has thrown into question any form of video evidence. In my experience with computers and even with video generating AI, it is hard for me to guess what's real and what's not from the clips that each side presented."

The room mulled over the idea that the police could arrest the wrong person. They went back and forth over the video evidence, eventually suggesting that it was useless.

Donna, the woman with the sour face, then brought up the DNA. She argued that DNA is harder to clean up than fingerprints, and so she held steadfast that Mr. Wilson killed the victim.

"What about the evidence from the bank?" Asked another juror.

"It could have been the last thing he did before getting on a plane. Remember, Atlanta is a different time zone, so he had more than three hours to commit the crime," Donna said, defending her idea.

"So how long would it take for a person to get to the airport, board a flight, fly across country, and leave the airport?"

Another juror, who had the look of a businessman chimed in, "That's also possible in theory. Usually that would take six to eight hours, but if he is using the new TSA pre-screening, he could get that down to four hours."

"Four hours is enough for him to actually commit the murder."

The jury looked around at each other. Some questions still lingered, but faced with going home tonight or continuing the debate, they settled on their answer that Mr. Wilson killed Jessie Vargus.

"I'll let the bailiff know," John said.

"Has the jury reached a verdict?"

"We have, your honor." John passed the paper to the bailiff.

"Will the defendant please rise?"

The courtroom bustled while Bobby Wilson stood.

"Bobby Wilson, the jury finds you guilty of the crime of second degree murder of Jessie Vargus. You will hereby be remanded into custody while you await your sentencing."

Bobby looked at his attorney and nodded in dejection. "Begin the appeals process, Mr. Gates. I am not guilty of this crime."

And he knew it in his heart.

In Your Dreams

I – The Protocol

noise echoed from every corner of the crowded lecture hall. Students had been filtering in for twenty minutes without instruction. Causal conversations between college-age men and women danced through the lecture hall. A few people came with friends, the rest wondered in alone for the hope of a few cookies perched just outside the door. The hundred dollar cash prize for selected participants provided further incentive.

Sara took in the sights, scribbling down notes of observations, the training from her journalism degree. She also thought that, as a columnist for the campus newspaper, a story might emerge from all this. She scanned the room for any of her friends, but didn't notice any at first glance.

Sara noticed an older man in a loosely fitting suit approach the podium that had previously sat lonely in center stage.

"Please quiet down now, folks."

The room silenced like a lecture was about to begin. What started as a noisy evening turned into the attention usually reserved for the midterm exams.

"My name is Dr. Philips. I will be the lead investigator on this project. I want to introduce to you my two assistants. Michelle is my post-doc fellow, and Jason, my graduate student. I trust you are all here in response to our call for participants in our next study. This is the Dream Study, where we will attempt to measure the effectiveness of sleep when placed inside a dream."

The students looked around at each other. One person raised their hand.

"Yes, sir?" Dr. Philips said, pointing to the student.

"What if we don't dream much?" The young man replied.

"Well, sir, this is a followup to our prior work that demonstrated the ability to induce dreams over eighty percent of the time. Now we are measuring the effectiveness of sleep on academic performance, health markers, and the like, while in an induced dream state."

Sara raised her hand next.

"Ma'am?"

"Thank you, Dr. Philips. How will you measure our health and academic performance?"

"I'm getting there, if I may continue."

She nodded to him and smiled.

"We will hand out some forms where we need to get your permission to monitor your health through a smartwatch, and your grades through your department. We will have some strict protocols about the time you get to sleep and the number of hours you achieve each night. If you regularly attend parties, you can excuse yourself at this point. We do not want the parties to influence us yet, but next semester we intend to perform a similar experiment for the party crowd, so please return next year for consideration in a similar study."

Several students stood up and gathered their belongings.

"Please help yourself to more cookies and coffee. We don't want any to go to waste."

Dr. Philips paused while the party crowd exited the room.

"Now, for those who remain, our study follows strict human review protocols, so you consent to our collecting limited health markers. We will supply you with a smartwatch that you will wear. It monitors heart rate, sleep time, and sleep state. It does not monitor or track your location. You will install an app on your phone and make sure to it connects to the watch. The app will transmit the data it collects over the day to our servers for study. We will not know who exactly has which watch. It is double-blind, limited participants for this first trial study."

He paused and looked around the room.

"Now, please excuse yourself if you do not consent to these guidelines."

A few more students trickled out of the room leaving about thirty people left.

"Now, I'll ask Jason for a brief demonstration of our equipment used to induce our dream state."

The student approached the podium with the same nervous apprehension many people have standing before crowds, especially as a young, untested graduate student. The bulky equipment resembling a VR helmet in his hand intensified his awkwardness.

"So, uh, everyone will wear a headset when they go to sleep at night. We will show you how to turn it on and connect it to your app. The device, uh, will connect to your brainwaves, and, uh, sync your brain with the frequency you need to dream."

"Thank you, Jason," Dr. Philips said, once again taking the podium. "So, if you would like to be considered for participation in the study, please stay behind, and we have a detailed experimental opt-in form."

After the remaining students trickled out, about twenty people remained and were interested in the study.

"OK, Michelle and Jason will hand out the forms. It is self-explanatory, but needs to be filled out in completion. We need your major, the names of any friends you have who are still in the room, all the consent forms filled out, and check that you agree to this thirty-day project, which you will see to the end."

II – The Dreams

Roger stretched out and breathed in the fresh air. The open window let in just the amount of air to freshen the day. Before fully opening his eyes, he grabbed the phone from the wireless charger on the nightstand.

A notification of a text message beeped at him once again as he opened the phone. He scrolled past it to the sleep monitor app. The science geek in him longed to see the data. He spent eight hours sleeping, two of it in REM sleep, and then he remembered the dream. It was pleasant, even sweet, though his macho man self would never admit that to anyone he knew.

The app opened up a pop-up window:

"How do you feel today?"

The answers were simple emojis, forcing him to sympathize with the sweet dream and click the drooling, happy button to indicate refreshing sleep.

"Do you remember your dream?"

Various cartoons depicted a range: yes, no, maybe. He picked the one in the middle. He knew he dreamed, and he had a sense in his heart that his dream was amazing, but he could not remember the details of the dream.

Roger scrolled through the various other statistics seeing what the heart rate looked like throughout the night in a chart. The screen displayed the bump in heart rate as associated with the time he dreamed. Makes sense, he thought, as his dreams often caused changes in his physical expressions.

Roger got up and prepared to leave for the classroom.

It was comforting, peaceful even. I remember vaguely the dream, but it is still slightly out of reach. It was peaceful in the woods, like when I was a child with my brother exploring the creek beds, looking for crayfish. The cool water flows through my hands. I can still smell the breeze bringing the soft aroma of maturing crab apples. I feel the warm sunshine on my flowing blond hair. It must have been a memory merging with a dream, right on the edge of consciousnesses. I remember so much…yet so little.

Sara looked at the words in her journal, softly smiling as she sipped her coffee, being aware that the steam could still burn her lips. She opened up the phone app, ready to answer the questions about the dreams and how she felt. She was not as interested in the statistics, so she answered the questions and moved on to the news app to analyze the writing style of the recent headlines.

Even before she wrote for the newspaper, this had been a habit of hers. She developed this habit of reading the same article from different perspectives in high school, a habit that influenced her journalism major. Sara wrote a few more lines, being satisfied with the results of her morning reflections.

"Hey, Roger, how'd you do?"

"Pretty good, I think. I'm confident I aced another."

"Of course you did. You're not known as the curve ball for nothing! Thanks for that studying help the other night. I hope that helped me out. I remembered a few more things from our session."

"Not a problem, Todd. We can do it again any time. Tutoring really helps me to understand the material better, myself, so the more I help others, the better I do myself."

The two men walked together to the fast food court attached to the dormitory on the far end of campus. They talked about the class, exam, and the cute girls in the class. Todd mentioned the party in his fraternity hall.

"Sadly, I can't go to a party for about a month. I'm in this sleep study at the psych department and one rule is not to party for the duration of the thirty-day study...but once the study is over, I'm there!"

"No partying for thirty days? What kind of torture is that? This is college. You're supposed to live it up!"

"Well, I've never been interested in parties much, anyway. But hey, next semester they are going to do the same study with people who are into partying. You can earn some extra cash."

"What's the study about?"

Roger detailed the purpose and procedure for the study, and that they were looking at sleep effectiveness and the induction of dreams.

By the time he was done with his explanations, they moved to the cashier.

"What's that?" Roger said, pointing to a can behind the counter.

"Oh," the cashier said, "Some new drink they are testing on campus. Want to try one?"

"Not today," he said. "I was just curious."

They paid and continued their conversation at the table before parting ways until the lab later that day.

Sara sat down at the table in the corner overlooking the walkway to observe the people walking by. She sipped her coffee on several days in the study, thinking about the dream. It was not the peaceful walk through the woods reminiscent of her childhood the previous night was. But it was still peaceful, just public. She sat at a table not too unlike this one, still writing in her journal and writing some news articles. But she couldn't quite place what she was drinking. It was not her regular coffee; she remembers that, but what she drank still eluded her. The memories of her dream compelled themselves to her paper.

> I love observing people. I observe them from afar. They
> don't know I'm looking, but I am. Everyone is addicted
> to smartphones, so they can't watch me observe them.
> They are not conscience of the staring. I rest on my
> perch in the corner booth, making my observations.
> Making up stories about them hones my craft. I sit there
> like a crazy person in this digitally saturated world, just
> drinking my coffee…my beverage of choice. I love
> coffee, always have. Ever since the first sip, on my first
> morning of high school, I loved coffee. But this dream
> was different. I was in my element, satisfied, observing
> people. But I didn't have my coffee. It was something
> strange, yet significant. Enough to remember, but not
> enough to remember perfectly. It is on my tip of my
> memory, yet eludes detection. What is it?

The words saturated the journal, making the impact as Sara looked through them, thinking. What was it?

Dreams are usually elusive, but to what end? She closed the book and looked out over to the walkway, seeing people walking in this direction or that. Some were clearly late for class, darting between the holes in the traffic. Others strolled without a care in the world. They must be off for the period. She focused on two men walking on the bridge toward the science section on campus. What could these two be talking about?

The breeze blew past Roger and Todd as they walked at a comfortable pace over the bridge. Suddenly, a rushing student brushed past them, running late for class. They looked at each other as the man almost knocked them into each other. They smiled and went on, realizing that the rushed student was once them on several occasions. It was too beautiful of a morning to be concerned about a man in a hurry.

"My dream last night was weird. Good, but weird," Roger said.

"How so? I never remember my dreams," Todd volunteered.

"I usually don't, but their device intensifies dreams, so we would remember. Something about the brain waves syncing with the device we wear at night when we sleep."

Roger paused for a moment, looking down over the pedestrian bridge to the grass below.

"I was at a party in this dream...probably your fault for inviting me to that party I can't attend."

Todd smirked.

"We weren't getting drunk. It was a dry party; no alcohol at all. Everyone drank the same thing, but a few different flavors. It was something distinct but unusual. You know how you have detailed dreams, but one thing is just outside of explanation? That was what we all drank. It was like something I might recognize if I saw it again, but nothing I would know to look for. But of course, it's kinda driving me nuts because after dreaming about it, I want some, but don't know what to buy!"

"Well, maybe you will see it for lunch after class? Are we going back to eat after the lecture?"

III – The Product

Very good, Sara. I love your use of language to get us to *feel* the senses as we travel through your stories."

"Thank you, Dr. Grasper."

Sara took her seat as small applause from the class echoed throughout the room. The next student already stood to read his piece.

Sara listened intently before catching a squirrel in the corner of her eye, mocking the students in the classroom. She looked out the window, thinking once again of the mystery vexing her in her dream. Her thoughts moved again to the mysterious can, then she snapped back into the attention when the classroom burst into applause. She clapped along, having missed most of the presentation.

The students scattered to the four corners of campus once class ended, and Sara went down to the cafeteria to work on some assignments. She moved through the line, grabbing a salad and fruit bowl. Making her way to the cashier when she looked up.

"I don't believe it," she said, just over audible.

"What?"

Sara snapped back to reality when the woman standing next to her spoke.

"What? Oh, nothing," she said.

The woman moved on.

Once Sara reached the cashier, she asked to see the can that was stacked up behind her.

"Oh, this one? Not sure what it is. We were just told to put it back here and sell it to anyone who wanted a can. It's three dollars."

"Oh. I guess I'll take it. You won't believe it, but I actually think this is something I was drinking in my dream last night."

"Interesting," the cashier said, placing the can on her tray. "That will be fourteen dollars on your meal card."

Sara slid her card through the payment kiosk and the screen flashed with a green check mark. She took her tray over by the window seat and studied the can.

The blue label was bland. It crossed her mind that the designer who made the can ought to be fired for producing such boring work. She scrolled to the nutrition label. The high sugar and high-fructose corn syrup suggested an excessively sweet drink, the kind she usually only consumed on special occasions.

She popped open the tab. A burst of carbonated air whispered through her corner as she caught the scent of a generic cola. She took a hesitant swig and set the can back down onto the table, absorbing all the flavors. The distinct cola flavor danced on her taste buds as she swallowed her overpriced drink.

"Three dollars for a bad coke." she smiled to herself. Yet the knowledge that this was the drink consuming her daydreams contented her, so she was free again to focus on her work.

Roger and Todd entered the cafeteria with the new wave of students. They laughed at small jokes between friends when Roger looked up and caught Sara's eye.

"Wait here a minute," he said, walking toward Sara.

Their eyes met, and Sara placed her pen down on the table.

"Hi," Roger said, introducing himself.

"I'm Sara," she returned.

Todd watched from afar, smiling and nodding his head in satisfaction.

"My buddy found a lady," he smirked to himself.

He watched them interact, unable to hear the conversation. He watched as he picked up the blue can to look at it, set it down, and pulled out his phone. It looked like they exchanged numbers. Roger smiled and turned back to Todd, seeing his friend grin from ear to ear.

"Found a lady?" he jabbed.

"Maybe. But what I really found is that drink she had. That's the one I mentioned, from the dream! Turns out we are both in the dream study, and both dreamed about this stuff. She said it takes like a generic cola. I'm gonna try one out."

Todd slapped his shoulder.

"Dude. You got her *number*. Ask her out!"

"I'll start with some coffee over the stories of dreams. Then see what happens from there."

Roger's phone beeped. A text message appeared on the home screen.

Sara:
Looking forward to the dream talk...

He smiled, reading the message, looked back up at her and raised his eyebrow. He shot back a quick reply:

Time tonight?

She broke her glance to look down at the phone, still smiling.

Any time after 7

They still glanced at each other, but he looked down.

Great, that works for me! Where?

He slid his phone back into his pocket and dragged Todd back to her table.

"Sara, this is my friend Todd. I figured I would introduce you guys, since he keeps assuming things."

"Nice to meet you Todd. I guess it's a good sign if a guy wants me to meet his friends."

"I'll take that as a compliment!" he said.

"If this works, we can both meet here by the doors at 7:15 tonight?"

Roger walked down the aisles at the grocery store, picking up a few random things that he could have in a dorm room on campus. Ramen noodles and popcorn were the first things in the basket, followed by a few breakfast bars and granola. He preferred proper foods, but access to a kitchen was very limited on campus.

Roger made a last turn down the beverage aisle looking for the drink he had for lunch, but the store didn't seem to carry it. He looked at his watch.

"Six." He said, "Plenty of time."

He made his way through the line at the store and finished putting away the groceries by 6:30. Roger sat at his table, set an alarm, and cycled through some flash cards to study before meeting Sara.

IV – The Meeting

Roger and Sara arrived at the cafeteria at the same time. Their eyes met and Roger reached for the door, allowing her in first.

At their table, coffee in hand, they described their dreams to each other. Roger recited from memory while Sara read her journal entry about it. They pondered it and stared at the single can they purchased, not to consume, but to ponder over. It just seemed right as they met over this thing.

"There were three, right?"

"Three?" Roger asked.

"Yes, three participants in each of the experimental groups. So in theory, one more person has probably purchased this drink. What if we take turns scoping out the cafeteria, waiting for someone else to have a can? Then we can ask if they are in the study?"

Roger nodded at the idea. He paused and then had another plan.

"I'll be right back," he said, standing up from the table.

Sara watched Roger stroll over to the cashier. He interrupted the cleaning of her nails, bored from the sparse clientele in the evening. Sara watched as they conversed. Roger pointed to the cans and appeared to be asking questions. The cashier bobbed her head back and forth in the conversation.

"Thanks," Roger said, walking back to the table and sliding into the booth.

"The cashier said that she only remembers one other person buying the drink more than once. A woman who is usually in for dinner."

"I'm never here for dinner," Sara said.

"Sara," Roger said, "Will you have dinner with me here tomorrow?"

They both chuckled.

"I'll have to ask my parents." She joked in return.

Dinner time in the cafeteria is bustling and loud. It reminded Roger and Sara why they had never eaten there after lunch. Still, they made their way through the line and found a small two-person table to sit at.

"The cashier said it was a woman we were looking for. Fortunately, the can sticks out like a sore thumb."

Roger scanned the room in his direction while Sara looked opposite him. She noticed a woman seated at a table with a few other students holding up the distinct blue can. The woman pointed to several places on it and spoke to her crowd. She then took a sip and made a cringing face, like she didn't like soda.

"I see her. At least someone with a can."

Roger turned around and confirmed a woman with the can, still holding it up and pointing to different parts on the label.

"I'll go over," she said, standing up. Roger watched her walk over.

The ladies conversed like ladies often do, freely, openly. They smiled at each other and both pulled out their phones. It looked like they were trading numbers. Then they nodded at each other, and Sara walked back to the table.

"It's her. She is an econ major, curious about why they released a product with such bad marketing. Her name is Sally, and we are meeting here tomorrow for lunch to get the story."

"I just put the finishing touches on my article this morning," Sara said, passing out a copy to Sally and Roger.

They both studied the paper. The title, "Dream Marketing" displayed prominently at the top. The table was quiet as the three read through the paper. Each one highlighted a few points of curiosity. Roger finished the paper first, setting it down and swigging from his coffee cup.

"It's a fascinating piece," Sally said. "You captured the essence of my dream perfectly. Boardroom meeting, critiquing the can, and even how I saw the can sitting there in the cafeteria, the can from my dream! I love it."

"The editor of the paper said it was a sure-fire inclusion of the paper, but to do so, it might damage the experiment. None of us were ever supposed to meet.

Maybe, though, it is good that we did. Maybe we even proved what they were 'really' trying to prove."

"Let's hold on to the paper until after the study, then release it," Roger said.

"My editor considered that, but thought that might not be the best thing to do from the standpoint of ethics."

"What if we just go to the psych department and talk to them? The study only has a week left," Sally suggested.

The three determined that was the best approach.

Roger knocked on the door. The Dr. Philips looked up from his computer screen, seeing three students crowded together at his door.

"Oh my goodness," he said, "Do you have questions about the exam?"

"No, sir. We are all part of the Dream Project. We are your experimental group, and we all met over an observation that we were the only ones who paid attention to that blue soft drink behind the counter of the cafeteria. That was the 'hidden' experiment, wasn't it?"

"Hidden experiment?"

"Yes," Roger said, "My older brother went to grad school for psychology. He said these studies usually have a hidden experiment that the test subject doesn't know about. This was about marketing to people in dreams, wasn't it?"

"Was it?" he mused.

"We believe so," Sara said. "All of us had the same dream behavior, which resulted in an observable real-world effect. We saw each other with the can, but no one else ever heard about it. As a journalist major, I had to write an article."

Sara opened the folder in her hand and handed the professor a draft. He sat back in his chair and scanned the pages.

"You are an excellent writer, Sara," he said. "Yes, the hidden experiment was to see if we could market products in simulated dreams. I trust the dreams related to something you usually like to do?"

Dr. Philips paused.

"Please don't answer that for me. I want the experiment to continue. Did you say this was going to be an article for the paper?"

"That was the intent, sir."

"That is fine with me...*if* you can wait for three weeks to publish it. It truly is a great article and I think people need to be aware of what can be done. I would like my student and post-doc to have the benefit of seeing if this result happened from the study organically. Is that acceptable?"

"Certainly, doctor."

"Great. If you can, please don't come as a group or pair for the final analysis."

The students all agreed to continue the experiment, but now knowing what the dreams tried to do, they resisted the marketing attempts.

Data Cell

I – Trade Track

"Grandma!" Bobby excitedly exclaimed, hitting the landing with all the muster a six-year-old could. He ran over into her outstretched arms.

They squeezed each other, and then Bobby squirmed his way out of her embrace.

"Whatcha you doing here?"

"Of course I wouldn't miss Track Day!"

"I hope I get to be a fireman!"

"Well, Bobby, as a little girl growing up in the old world, teachers *asked* us what we *wanted* to be when we grew up."

"Mom, you know it's not like that anymore. If everyone got to choose what they wanted to do, we wouldn't have people to do the gross jobs. No one wants to be a garbage man. You know that."

"That's true, dear, that people don't dream of being the garbage man, but I noticed I never had a week when a garbage man *didn't* show up! Sometimes the garbage man was just a person without a plan."

Debbie looked her mom up and down and then glanced at Bobby as he stirred his cereal.

"Bobby, you need to hurry and finish. We don't want to be late!"

Bobby overfilled his mouth and drops of cereal fell out as he chewed.

"Close your mouth to eat," she admonished.

Grandma spoke again of the older ways. "We used to do aptitude tests to know what to improve on. We didn't use it to put a six-year-old on a certain track and keep him there for the rest of his life."

"Well, Mom. Times have changed. The New Founders assign what we will do. I just hope he is on the blue-collar track, so we don't have to worry about his education separating the family by ideology."

"Well, Debbie," she countered, "Another thing we *should* be doing at home and not in the school system. It should be up to the parents to raise a kid into ethics, not the school system or the Data Cell they are assigned to."

"I can agree that I wish we had more input into his moral upbringing, but it's still not our business to try overriding the Track the system places us on. You know that."

"I am reminded every time I look at Bob's picture that I should not disparage another person's Track. But that hardly makes it ethical!"

"Society defines ethics, Mom, you know that."

"It didn't always," she retorted.

Bobby jumped up from the table and ran a few circles around the dog, who watched as if preparing to chase his own tail.

"Get your shoes on. We gotta go!"

We want to welcome you all to Track Day! As you know, the New Founders created Track Day to balance our society. Some people need to assist the machines, and others need to fix them. In the old world we had a thing called, "unemployment" that happened when people couldn't find work. That happened because the old, dangerous ideas led our society's leaders to let people choose their own occupations. This meant that too many people wanted the glamorous jobs, and no one wanted to be garbage collectors.

The New Founders first tackled unemployment by making sure every task in society was assigned a person best fit for the role. Track Day is when the aptitude tests our students have been working so hard on assign their Track that moves them into the academic, thought, and moral process needed to complete the task they are assigned to work on during their lifetime. It is a system balanced and perfected by Artificial Intelligence. As your school superintendent, it is my honor to welcome you to this district's Track Day.

The six-year-old class sat on stage behind Mr. Connor, wiggling away as young kids are so inclined to do. The teachers corrected the most distracting behavior, but let the minor offenses go. Bobby sat next to Jenny, quietly talking about their hopes. Bobby repeated the desire to be a fireman while Jenny hoped her task would be a teacher.

"Robert Miles."

Bobby jumped up and ran with enthusiasm to the podium. He dashed through the biometric data collection, providing a fingerprint, iris scan, and voice sample to the computer. He hesitantly approached the woman in the white coat with his finger extended. She wiped it down with a white scrub pad and pricked his finger, smearing the blood sample on the card before feeding it into the computer for analysis. He sucked his finger before being reprimanded to select a bandage instead.

"Robert Miles is assigned to the blue collar track of HVAC technician. He will soon be a person keeping our buildings comfortable for everyone. Congratulations, Robert." Mr. Connor said as Bobby made his way back to his chair.

"Jennifer Morgan."

Jenny ran up with the same childlike enthusiasm as Bobby and ran through her battery of identification protocols.

"Jennifer Morgan is assigned to the white collar track of office finance manager. This important role requires a battery of college courses, and then finally she will be ready to keep accounting in line for one of several companies that keep our society running. We have a short list to share with her family soon."

Mr. Conner assigned the remaining students their tracks and let the festivities commence as the various relatives talked up their tracks to the kids, most of whom were rejected from the dreams of their future careers.

"What is an HVAC Technician?" Bobby asked when reunited his mom.

"He repairs the thing outside the house on that side you are not allowed to play on. Sometimes they break and need fixed. It will be so handy having an air conditioner repairman in the family!"

Bobby looked at his feet and sighed, "I wanted to be a fireman!" he said, pouting off into an empty corner. Debbie looked around the room, seeing many other kids expressing similar emotions, but she knew it was futile, as once the computer decided your track, you would be on that track without exception.

II – Growing Up

Bobby stood in front of the mirror teasing his hair to utter perfection.

"Bobby, are you almost ready?"

"Yeah, mom!" he yelled from upstairs, still pimping his appearance out in the mirror, perfectly styling his hair for the first day of high school.

He thought back to his last day of middle school and how some of his old friends had to part ways now to focus on the career tracks assigned by the AI. A small tear formed when he remembered his best friend growing up was on a different Track, so the system required separation as he went to a high school for blue-focus while his friend went off to the white-focus school.

He wiped away the tear and put on a frown, remembering he still had friends joining him this year for his Track studies. His school pushed more conservative ideas, providing a minor push-back against the progressive change that sometimes went too far. His best friend went to a school focused entirely on college prep and then giving him the groundwork for his Track career.

It was impossible to push against the system.

He glanced again, satisfied with the position of the last few strands of hair, and switched off the light.

"Is my backpack down there?" He yelled out from the upper banister.

"Yes, it's prepped up and at the door. Come down for your breakfast!"

Robert ran down the stairs with the final mustered excitement as the little child gave way to the budding adult instead. Still, he jumped down the final stairs, hitting the floor with a massive THUD!

"You're not six anymore, Bobby."

"I know. I was just trying to remember how it was to be a kid. You know Mike is going to the other school, right?"

"Yes, I remember that. But you have some other friends closer to your Track, right?"

"None in my complete Track, but I have some friends in the blue-collar sector, so I guess there's that."

Robert ate cereal, more like a man now, being cautious of too much on the spoon and not spilling. The summer saw his adolescence blossom, and he released the angst of a forced career out of his system by rebelling before society would be too hard on him. He resigned himself to his assigned position.

"Good morning everyone. I trust you had a great summer and are back rested and ready to learn."

The video announcements gave the early morning welcomes and instructions, mostly useful to the incoming freshman class.

"During this first week, everyone will need to come down to the technology office to re-scan your biometrics. We don't need anyone locked out of your Data Cell by a summer growth spurt. Of course, you may have updated your biometrics already if our devices instructed you to over the summer. You still need to come to the tech office to provide the confirmation in our system of that change."

Robert had already updated his biometrics. His summer rebellious streak gave him a week of retraining. His crime was simple: he looked up websites about opposing views and read them over, trying to understand why people thought differently than he did. Such reading could pollute his Data Cell, so the AI flagged him to report to retraining where they purged his Data Cell of his summer misadventures. If the cell didn't get purged, the system might feed him more information opposed to his Track and that could lead to a free thinker...the bane of society.

Since he hit a growth spurt, the retraining program already re-scanned and cleaned his Data Cell. They notified the school, and Robert would be on the watch list to more heavily scrutinize the things he saw on his devices.

"PSSTT," a boy sounded, looking for Robert's attention.

He turned and looked at the somewhat familiar face.

"Yeah?"

"You were at retraining, weren't you?"

"Yeah. That's where I recognize you from."

"I thought so. What lunch do you have?"

Robert flipped through his schedule, looking for the lunch period.

"C," he finally said.

"I do, too. Let's look for each other."

Lunch in high school is not nearly as terrifying as it was in middle school. While the middle schoolers are trying to prove themselves, the high school class resigned themselves to their role in life. They just sat down with kids from their classes if they didn't see friends at first glance.

Today he was looking for someone in particular.

"John!" Robert yelled from across the dining hall.

"Robert! We saved you a seat!" John motioned, pointing to a seat next to him.

Robert walked over with his tray and set it down.

"Boys, this is another retrainie."

"Yo," "Yo", "YOOO," the guys at the table all took turns saying.

"We have all been to retraining. Even here, they try to watch us more closely. So, have you been...reformed?" John asked.

"Well, I can say that I have accepted my fate, but I still can't get this nagging curiosity out of my mind. I am just terrified of being vanished to look into it more." He said, not sure what caused him to be so open upon strangers.

"We are all curious, and we have some solutions, but we don't want to talk about it here. What sector do you live in?"

"F block," Robert said.

"You know the old vine patch at the top of the hill?"

"Yeah, I know it."

"We meet up there on Wednesdays after school."

Curiosity and fear gripped Robert on his walk up the hill. He thought this new group of friends could be spies, helping to determine if he was properly retrained or not. The New Founders often deployed spies around retrainies, but he never met one in real life...that he was aware of.

Still, he visited the vine patch often enough to be there by coincidence, so he checked it out.

His pulse increased as he approached the patch. He walked in by the solitary trail, through the thin walls of small shrubbery, into a wide open mature forest with several vines hanging down. As preteens, he and his friends would come here to swing on the vines to escape the summer boredom. One was a long ride spanning the whole open area from front to back. Another, a small, quick vine that gave enough g-force to fall off if you weren't careful. Other natural rides were also present in the place.

He remembered the former echos of his friends but stood at the entrance, scanning the scene. He heard a stick break beside him, causing him to dart his attention to the sound. John approached with his finger over his mouth, making a 'shush' motion. He held an old tin box in his hand, something like Robert once saw at his grandmother's house.

John opened the tin and motioned it toward Robert. It had a few cell phones in it.

"Put yours in," he whispered.

Not knowing why, Robert put his cell phone into the box and John sealed it up.

Returning to his normal voice, John explained, "The tin box blocks the phone's signals. The phone can't hear us or report our location when in here. We need to join the guys at our hangout."

John led them down a few difficult to find paths and finally to a hollowed out bush where all the guys from the lunch table sat in folding chairs.

"This is our hideout. It's free of the tracking and listening our devices constantly do. We can talk freely here and wonder about what the world's like on the forbidden side. Rule: Your phone must never come here without being placed in a metal box. We don't want our phone locations to trigger us being here. We don't want the microphones to hear what we talk about. Got it?"

"Yes." Robert said.

"Great. Now, if you are still curious about the other side, I have a tool you can borrow."

"What is it?"

"Here," John tossed him a square block of tinfoil, "Don't open it here."

"What is it?" Robert asked again.

"That's the answer to your questions. Have you ever heard of TWAR?"

Robert looked at him and squinted, momentarily pondering if he should lie to sound smarter than he was, or if he should just get all the information. He didn't need to answer, since his face confessed his ignorance.

"TWAR stands for Track Shift Data Cell Research, a tool that lets us look at the Internet from either cell position. Our Data Cell is locked to our biometric data, so when we turn it on, we only see the Internet from the perspective of our assigned cell. This does not use biometrics, and it allows you to choose what type of data cell you view the Internet from. Even the New Founders version of the Internet. It will answer all your questions."

Robert silently processed his thoughts. He longed to see the world outside his assigned cell, but he was afraid of suffering the fate of his grandfather. He tossed it back to John.

"Is it OK if I think about it?"

III – A Chance Encounter

Robert sat at the counter scrolling through news feeds. Each article he saw made him shake his head in disgust about the direction the world headed. The left wing crazies were protesting again about the latest outrage, seething in their shouts about things that didn't even make any sense to him. But he knew why they thought the way they had.

He massaged his lower lip, trying to imagine what a piercing there might feel like. He ran his tongue over the backside of the lip and shook his head over the crazy protest.

A text message from John made him chuckle. The picture displayed a protester with a pithy caption that would certainly be called racist by the White Trackers. He shook his head and then forwarded the message to his dad. He set the phone down and picked up the coffee, taking a sip while glancing around.

Robert noticed a pretty young woman a few seats over, and he thought he recognized her.

"You're Jenifer, right?"

"I am. Bobby, is that you?"

"It is! I haven't seen you in a while. Our last classes were in the seventh grade, then our tracks diverged." He paused. "I saw you at lunch a few times before we were shipped to different schools," he said.

"So what Track you are on?" She asked, making conversation.

Robert slid over to the empty stool between them and finally answered.

"I'm on track for HVAC Technician. Pretty good job field and I start after only one year of training after we graduate."

"Nice," she said. "I am doomed to six more years of schooling. They assigned me to finance marketing and control work. An office job."

"That's great. That means you must be pretty smart."

Jenifer thought about that question and pondered if it was her brains or just her hard work that pushed her to that track. She remembered her parents pushed her really hard to pass the Track tests, a decision she has wrestled with since being first assigned the track.

"I'm not sure. I'm still not that great with numbers… and they say it will be my career. Sometimes I wonder if who we are doesn't determine our track as much as how hard parents pushed us as kids."

She described the push her parents gave her to give up many childhood games to pursue passing the tests. In her household, only the college degree jobs were credible. Anyone that didn't go to college was just an imbecile. A way of thinking they did their best to instill in her.

"They would really love me. My teachers all say that I was mis-assigned because apparently I'm pretty smart, but I am only trained on the basics. I won't have the opportunity to go to college. But honestly, I'm not sure if I would want to go, anyway."

"Why not?" she retorted.

"I see college is all about the 'experience' and not the learning, yet you need to get that 'experience' to get your job in your track. But it doesn't look like experience in the field…just experience in socializing."

Jenifer thought about that but felt the urge to defend her push to attend college.

"Well, what I see on my news feeds is that people on the blue collar track repeatedly drink a lot of beer and make racist jokes about everyone they don't look like."

Robert took his turn, thinking of his response. Thanks to his years of research on TWAR, he knew the ideologies pushed them into pre-planned thought processes, though he knew more truths about society's induced reality.

"You know what's interesting here?" He said.

"What?" she said, still sounding defensive.

"I have never had the chance to see the articles you see," he lied, "and you have never seen the articles I see. I wonder if the actual truth is somewhere in between."

But he knew that the truth was in between the two poles the system constantly forced the students into believing.

"We are just too different to come to any more understanding of each other. I just know I can't interfere with you fixing my air conditioner," She said.

"Yes. But if we want to understand each other, don't we need to have something in common? What if the computer has intentionally set our worlds apart to keep us from coming together to question who is in charge of this system?"

Jenifer thought about this. Her attraction to this handsome young man became intensified by his intelligence, particularly jarring since her whole upbringing taught her that Blue Trackers were shallow idiots, but necessary for the basest components of society.

"What do you propose?" She asked.

"Let's try to understand each other."

"How?"

Robert devised a plan. If she saw that the same news organizations printed completely contrary articles for each track, she might see that someone must be manipulating the information the people use in forming their opinions on many societal matters.

"Johnny!" He called out.

The white-suited diner manager peeked out of the door to the kitchen.

"Whatcha need?"

"Just letting you know we are moving to a booth over there."

"Cool thing, kids." He smiled, shaking his head at a possible budding romance.

They slid into the booth, and Robert explained what he learned about algorithms. He explained that every news source and social media connected to their biometrically secured Data Cell and that the cell directed the content they could see.

"So what you are saying is that our applications don't even allow us to look for an article if it does not align with our Track?"

"Correct. So if you pull up the Daily Digest and search for this article, 'Protesters are at it again', you will probably not find it on the platform at all. Even though I see it in my feed now."

Jenifer pulled out her phone and searched in the Digest for the article, and it turned out empty. She then looked at her feed and read off an article title.

"Look for 'Legislators pass annual funding'," she said.

Robert confirmed he found it, but noted that the article is not a track story. The news kept people from finding out these differences in the spin by reporting some articles exactly to each track. He suggested finding something about a racist event, and they found an article she saw, but he didn't.

"So what's important is what is in these articles that seek to divide us. I'll read mine, word for word, without commentary, and what I want you to do is tell me what is true and what's not about the story. Obviously, we should jointly know the basics about a protest, but why they protest and what they are doing will probably be different. Let's find common ground."

IV – The Stories That Divide

Robert and Jenny took turns reading from their track stories and explaining to each other the points of view the system taught them about each other. At once, they realized their respective peer groups only hated each other because the system trained them in that hate.

"What can we do about it?" she said.

"There's not much we can do about it other than treat everyone with respect and understand they may not like us because of their conditioning." Robert said.

Jenny looked into his eyes and shook her head.

"What?" He asked.

"All my life I've been told how stupid people from your track are, yet you are brilliant. Is there hope for us?"

"The laws don't forbid us from dating, if that's what you're asking."

"My parents will hate this," she said.

"NO, JENNY!" Her dad yelled at the top of his voice.

"BUT WHY?" she countered.

"I WANT YOU MARRYING SOMEONE SMART!"

Jenny looked into her dad's eyes and fought for choice. She nodded at his declaration and lowered her voice, remembering from her psychology courses that it might calm the tone.

"He is smart. He is way smarter than the boys in my Track. I will insist on you meeting Robert before I will listen to any more of your advice."

"She's right, Jeff," her mom said, finally speaking up in the conversation.

Jeff exchanged glances between the two women and resigned himself to defeat. "Fine. Invite him to dinner, but my decision will not change. You need to find someone in the White Track, and not waste your time on these beer guzzling racists."

"Jeff, at least be reasonable."

"When I am in the company of reasonable people, I will be reasonable." He barked his words to cover the wounds of defeat and slammed the door as he walked into the garage.

"So, is your whole family Blue Track, Robert?" Jennifer's mother asked.

He nodded his head yes while swallowing a portion of corn. "Yes, ma'am. My dad's a car mechanic and my mom worked as a repair woman for textile manufacturing."

"And what is your selected area?"

"I will be an HVAC Technician. I only need one more year of schooling, and then I will work for the Starling Corp doing installs and occasional maintenance for the local high-rises." He paused, catching an evil eye from Jeff before continuing.

"And what do you folks do?" Addressing his question to Mrs. Morgan instead of Jeff.

"Well, Jeff is an office manager at Redstone and I do administrative assistant for another office manager there. Lots of school."

"That makes us smart, Robert. Do you know what that means?" Jeff snarled.

"Well, sir," Robert started, trying to read the room for how to proceed, "I know that college can teach excellent skills for good jobs…but I also know that my Track also requires specialized training and skills. We go to school for that."

"But my college has taught me a lot about the arts and the things of passion."

"A good sonnet is good, sir. I have heard many…but a sonnet has never kept your house cool in the summer."

"What do you know of sonnets?" Jeff said.

"Honey." Jennifer's mother said, looking at Jeff with a woman's evil eye.

"Well, what do these Bluies ever know of the arts? They just get their minimum school and go find life in cold beer."

Jeff stood up and wiped his mouth before throwing his napkin at the table and storming off.

"Sorry, Robert," Jennifer said. "He is so pig-headed sometimes."

"Jennifer!" her mother corrected.

"What? Robert is smarter than anyone in my classes. But Daddy will not even give him a chance to prove himself worthy."

"Worthy of what, dear?"

Robert bounced his head between the two women like he was watching the ball in a ping-pong match.

"Maybe it's not worth it," he finally said.

Jennifer went quiet and stood up.

"Excuse me," she said, wiping her eyes. She walked out of the room, leaving Robert and Mrs. Morgan alone in the room.

"I'm sorry," he said, standing up.

"Please. Sit back down." She started. "Jennifer is right about her father. He is pig-headed at times. He wants the best for his daughter...but I know she would not have invited you over here if there wasn't more to you than your handsome smile. If you like Jennifer, don't let Jeff get in your way. I'll talk to him."

They looked at each other for another eternity before Mrs. Morgan pointed down the hall.

"Second door on the right. Go talk to her."

He stood back up and walked down the hall, knocking on the door. She opened it up and shut the door behind him.

"You are worth it. I just don't want there to be a conflict with your father. But I am willing to muscle through it. You're smart, pretty, and the girl I always had a crush on growing up."

Jennifer looked up at him, and a slow smile grew on her face. "Is that true? You had a crush on me?"

"Yep. I was too afraid as a middle school kid to talk to you. Then, of course, our paths diverged in high school. When I saw you at the diner the other day, I thought that the world had given me another chance. So I took it."

"I'm glad you did, little Bobby. I want to make it work…with or without my dad's blessing."

Six months later, Robert reached into his secret stashing place for his unmonitored phone and turned it on. He switched on the TWAR network and started perusing the stories the system fed to the White Track group. The contrast between those and the stories on the blue track showed him how much society tried to pit the two groups against each other. He thought about Jeff and how the man hated him because of the stories he read about the blue track in his daily news feed. The system properly conditioned the man to hate him because of who he was assigned based on the computer and not who he was as a person.

He picked up his notebook and started scribbling notes. He wrote down some random thoughts and then picked up a fresh piece of paper and penned a letter.

Dear Jennifer,

The last six months have been the best of my life. I want to be with you always. I realized today, as I looked at the news we both can see, that your dad hates me because the system trained him to hate me. Nothing I have done created this behavior, and until he can set that aside and get to know me, he will keep hating me.

That being said, I am not ready to wait for him to change. He may never change, and I will be the big man who does not hold it against him. That is not him. This is the dualistic society the new founders created when they put artificial intelligence in charge of every decision. We can't do anything about that.

But we can start living life together. I want to marry you, if you will have me, and maybe together, we can raise children who can see everyone for who they are instead of what group they belong to. I hope you say yes.

Love,

Little Bobby

Acknowledgments

This project is the fruition of years of analyzing the news and presenting the technical goings-on of the world. I would not have kept up with the world events without the viewers on my videos on SwitchedToLinux. The idea to produce the stories in this book came from the many financial supporters who have supported my work through Patreon, Subscribestar, Locals, and ThinkLifeMedia. Thank you for your support.

I would also like to thank my many other friends who submitted ideas, provided insight on content, and performs proofreading and concepts. Thanks specifically to Deb, Patrick, Solbu, Yvon, and Dan for the most and direct input into several of the stories.

About the Author

Thomas Murosky started his career as a Chemistry professor, but stepped out of academia in 2010 to focus on other projects. Since that time, he has worked as a freelance technology consultant focusing on Internet privacy, FOSS software, and web design. He has founded a small Indie press where he publishes Christian living and science fiction. Tom is also the author behind the SwitchedToLinux brand which has helped several people understand the power of free and open source software in regular work routines.

Thomas Murosky has also written the science fiction novel Synaptergy, in addition to several Christian titles.